Judge Birdie #3

Ghost Island Mystery

Kirsten Usman

Judge Birdie #3
Ghost Island Mystery

Copyright © **2019 by Kirsten Usman**
Find out more at: www.PlanetProtector.com

PLANET
PROTECTOR
PUBLISHING

ISBN: 978-1-7324756-1-8
First Printing: April 2019

How much better to get wisdom than gold,

to get insight rather than silver.

Proverbs 16:16

Chapter 1

"Milo, we are going to be wickies!" I exclaimed. I raised my arms up in the air with triumph, my hands in tight fists.

Milo leaned across the table and whispered, "Grammy, I love to play pretend too but this might not be the best time." His eyes darted back and forth, looking at the nearby diners with embarrassment. Apparently my excitement was contagious because all the patrons of the café were staring at me wondering why I was so excited.

I smiled at the other customers and took a sip of my pink lemonade. "I am not playing pretend.

Though that does sound like fun! A wickie is a nickname for a lighthouse keeper. I just signed up to be a wickie for one month and I want you to come with me!"

"What are you talking about? A lighthouse keeper? You have a job. You are a judge, remember?" Milo picked up a packet of ketchup and spun it around in wild circles on the table, seemingly more interested in playing with the ketchup than my proposed adventure.

"I know I have a job but this opportunity arose and I could not pass it up. Lady Gray has been the lighthouse keeper on Ghost Island for the past fifty years. Unfortunately, she recently disappeared."

Milo stopped playing with the ketchup packet and looked at me with concern, so I continued. "The Park Patrol discovered that she was missing when they delivered her food and supplies. They found her tea cup still full and a few cookie crumbs on a plate on the kitchen table."

"WHAT?!? That's crazy! Do you think she is okay? Do you think they will find her?" Milo asked. "Oh, man, maybe a ghost ate her!"

"I don't know what happened. Maybe she got tired of her job, jumped on a boat and sailed away without telling anyone she quit!" I replied with a hopeful sigh. "Oh, and I am pretty sure ghosts don't eat things because ... well ... they are dead." I took a bite of my cheese pizza, savoring the gooey cheese and the crisp, crunchy crust.

"Anyway, the Park Patrol needs someone to help out until they find Lady Gray or hire a permanent replacement. This is a once in a lifetime opportunity that I could not let slip away. So, I immediately volunteered!"

"It sounds dangerous and scary. Ghost Island? Isn't that place haunted?" Milo asked. He took a bite of his grilled cheese sandwich and wiped his hands on his blue cloth napkin.

"You can't let fear stop you from living life!

Besides, you know that we are exceedingly capable of handling the unexpected after our last adventure," I said as I thought back to our recent camping trip.

A few months ago, Milo and I went on a camping and canoeing trip down the Greenville River. We encountered many unexpected problems along the way but we never gave up. We completed our trip successfully and learned many life lessons along the way.

Milo is my recently turned eight-year-old grandson and he is usually excited to come along on adventures with me. Though, from time to time, he does think my proposals are a bit unusual.

I am a federal court judge and typically very busy. However, a case set for trial settled and I had a break in my schedule so I immediately jumped on this extraordinary opportunity to temporarily work on Ghost Island.

"I will think about it," Milo said, skeptically.

"You can have about five minutes to think it over because … well … you see … we have to leave tomorrow morning," I said with a smile.

"Tomorrow morning? Grammy, I am supposed to go evidence hunting tomorrow. We still have not figured out who or what has been draining the Greenville River," Milo said.

At the end of our camping and canoeing trip, Milo and I discovered that the Greenville River was drying up before it reached the ocean. Upon returning home, we commenced our detective work and tried to solve the mystery. So far we have gathered very little evidence. Milo collected water and mud samples to inspect under his microscope. He found a blue thread in one of the samples. He also discovered a decomposing banana peel on the muddy riverbed. That didn't tell us much but he is determined to find out who or what was responsible.

"I knew you would not be happy having to leave

the mystery unsolved so I put an announcement in the newspaper. It declares that whoever solves the Greenville River mystery shall receive a $100 reward. So, you can take a break from your detective work and come with me!" I exclaimed.

Milo dipped his crispy French fries into the ketchup on his plate. "I guess it sounds like a fun adventure so … okay … I will go with you. Besides, somebody has to make sure you don't get yourself into too much trouble."

"Excellent!" I exclaimed. "I knew I could count on you!" I ate the last bite of my pizza and picked up the dessert menu.

"But I have one condition. When we get back you have to promise me that you won't sign up for any more adventures for at least two weeks," Milo said.

"One week," I said with a mischievous smile.

"Fine. One week. One whole week of peace at home," Milo said as he dug in his backpack. He pulled out an orange notebook and a pencil covered with green trees. "What should I bring?"

"We can't bring much," I said. "The lighthouse is only accessible by zip line from a boat. We are allowed one backpack each. The Park Patrol will provide us with food and supplies."

"One backpack? Zip line?" Milo sounded like I was speaking a foreign language.

"Yep, one backpack. Remember, the more stuff you have, the more stuff you have to take care of. This will be good for us. We will learn to do with less. We are going to find out that less really is more! And as for the zip line, well, we will figure it out. How hard could it be?"

"Oh, Grammy, where do you come up with this stuff? Why can't we be like everyone else? They are doing normal things like going for walks, doing puzzles, playing games, and going out to eat. Us? We go zip lining to a haunted island where we have to fight off monsters, ghosts and goblins. This is nuts, absolutely nuts!" Milo bit his lip and began to write his list on a new page in his notebook.

1. underwear
2. bathing suit
3. shield and sword so I can fight off the monsters and ghosts
4. my favorite buddies: wholly mammoth, porcupine, baby panda
5. a 10,000-piece puzzle so I don't get bored

"While you work on your list, let's order some dessert," I suggested, handing Milo the menu. "I think we should celebrate our last day on the mainland with a brownie sundae."

"Since we may not make it back and this could be our last day ever on the mainland, I think we should order a brownie sundae and the key lime pie," Milo said with a grin.

"Good idea. In fact, since it is unlikely that we will have any dessert on the island, I think we should also get two giant chocolate chip cookies. It's not as though we can get ingredients at a grocery store to make our own dessert or order some from a restaurant, for that matter." My thoughts began to swirl around the adventures that lie ahead. "Make sure to stuff a cholate bar or two into your backpack. For emergences!" I said, smiling.

Chapter 2

Usually Milo is the one waking me up in the morning, demanding we get going and start our day. But today I found myself pounding on his front door, in the dark, and yelling so loudly that I think I woke up the entire neighborhood.

"Milo, we are going to miss the boat! Get up! We have to go right now!"

A few moments later, Milo slowly opened the door. His light brown hair was disheveled, looking as though he had just crawled out of bed. He was wearing his favorite panda pajamas and holding his stuffed baby panda bear. Milo loves pandas and his current dream job is to work on conservation efforts to save them from extinction when he is an adult.

"It is still dark outside and it is pouring rain," Milo said while rubbing his eyes.

"A little rain never hurt anyone," I said. I shook the water off my yellow umbrella before stepping into the entryway.

"I need a few minutes to change out of my pajamas. And I better give my mom a kiss and hug goodbye or she will be on the next boat to the island. I know she can't survive without my kisses and hugs."

I scanned the bookshelves in Milo's living room while I waited for him to get ready. My eyes stopped on a book titled *Beware of Ghost Island*. I paged through the book and found it full of frightening ghost stories. Unexplained fires, moving rocking chairs, banging doors, and disappearing people were just some of the evidence seemingly proving that a real ghost lives within the lighthouse.

As I was reading a story claiming that a sea captain saw a girl in white floating around the top of the lighthouse, I heard Milo springing down the stairs. I slammed the book closed and hastily pushed it back in place on the bookshelf, secretly wishing I had never read it. Just as I got it back in place, Milo ran into the living room dragging an overflowing backpack. It was stuffed so full that the zipper barely closed.

I quickly composed myself and hoped my goosebumps wouldn't give me away. "Let me carry that for you, sweetie," I said, my voice quivering. "It looks a bit heavy. Oh my! What did you pack in here? Rocks?" I could barely pick it up. With two hands I slung it onto my back.

"I packed a couple of rocks, but only a few of my very favorite ones that I can't be without," Milo said matter-of-factly.

Milo raced through the pouring rain and jumped into the back seat of my green car. I put his backpack next to mine in the trunk before getting into the driver's seat.

"I thought you might not have time for breakfast this morning, so I whipped up a batch of your favorite pumpkin muffins," I said as I reached for a container on the passenger seat and handed it back to Milo.

"All right! My favorite muffins!" Milo exclaimed. Specks of the cinnamon sugar topping sprinkled to the floor as he pulled out the biggest muffin he could find. Then he sat back and munched on it as we drove away from his house.

As we made our way to the docks where the boat was going to pick us up, we watched the city slowly start to come to life. Store owners opened their shops, turning on lights and switching on the open signs in the doorways. We passed a woman out for a run and a police officer heading into the

Greenville Diner for breakfast.

At the docks we found a medium-sized white speedboat waiting for us. It had red racing stripes down the sides and the captain's chair was partially enclosed and protected. Thankfully, the rain was now just a slight, cool drizzle.

"Good morning," the captain said as we approached. He had a full white beard and short gray hair. He was wearing a yellow rain suit and a navy blue baseball cap.

"Good morning. My name is Birdie and this is my grandson, Milo."

"Nice to meet you. My name is Captain Hook."

Milo grabbed my hand and froze. He pulled on my arm, trying to get me to turn and run for our lives. "Captain Hook? The Captain Hook?"

"My last name is Hook, but no, I am not The Captain Hook. My name is James. James Hook. People ask that all the time. One year, I really scared some folks when I dressed up as a pirate for

Halloween. They were sure I was a real pirate for years after that. It was so much fun! But, I am sorry to have to say that I am not. I am simply the captain of this beautiful boat that I call Speed Racer."

Looking relieved, Milo climbed onto the boat and began exploring every nook and cranny.

"Where do the stairs lead to?" Milo asked excitedly as he peered into the darkness.

"Feel free to explore my boat," the captain said. "There is a small bed down there, some extra clothes, and a bit of food. Sometimes I go on long overnight trips and anchor at different islands."

Milo bounded down the stairs and disappeared while I slowly climbed on board. I really did not want to start our adventure with me falling into the ocean while attempting to get into the boat. Though that would be tremendously amusing for Milo, it was not an experience I wished to have.

"So, have you ever been a lighthouse keeper before?" the captain inquired. He took a seat cushion off of a bench, revealing a hidden compartment. Then he gestured for me to place our backpacks inside.

"Nope, first time for me!" I said, sounding a bit more enthusiastic than necessary.

Picking up on my nerves, the captain said, "Don't worry, you will be fine. And if you need anything, you can radio me and I will be there in a jiffy." He closed the lid, placed the seat cushion back on top, and gave it a push to ensure it was secure.

"Oh, that is so good to hear," I said with relief. "I was a little nervous when the Park Patrol told me I could not bring my cell phone with me."

"You can bring it but it won't be of much use because there isn't any service on the island," the captain said. "But, there is a CB radio at the lighthouse so you can reach me anytime. Lady Gray and I have talked many times over the years. She never had any emergencies but she liked to call and chitchat once in a while. I suppose it might get a little lonely being by yourself all the time." The captain sat down behind the steering wheel and fiddled around with the controls.

Milo finished exploring the lower deck and ran up the stairs and joined us. "Are there any other secret rooms on your boat?"

"No, I am afraid not," the captain said with a smile. "But I bet you will find some on the island! I have heard that there are secret rooms in the lighthouse. And supposedly there is a hidden treasure somewhere on the island. Even I have searched for it once or twice."

Deep in thought, Milo sat down in a seat at the back of the boat. I sat down right next to him so I could keep my hands on him, just in case it got a little bumpy.

"What do you think happened to Lady Gray?" I asked the captain.

"I don't know, but I hope she is okay. We talked

over the radio the night before she disappeared and it sounded like something was bothering her. I asked her if everything was alright and she said it was."

"I bet a ghost ate her!" Milo said.

"I have been to the island many times and I have never seen a ghost," the captain said. "But, one time as I navigated away, the lights at the top of the lighthouse flashed on and off at least twenty times. I radioed Lady Gray, thinking she needed me for something, but she said she wasn't blinking the lights. We never did find out what happened that day."

The captain handed us two bright orange life jackets. I helped Milo fasten his before putting on my own.

"The rain has slowed down so we better get going because it looks like it is supposed to pick up again shortly," the captain said. He unwound the ropes that tied Speed Racer to the dock and pulled the buoys back inside the boat. "Hopefully the water won't be too choppy."

The captain revved the engine and motored away from the dock. I watched civilization slowly disappearing behind us, feeling both excitement and anxiety for what was to come.

Soon we were out on the open ocean. The waves crashed against our boat sending sprays of salty sea water over us. Milo and I were soaked almost instantly. Every time our boat flew over a huge wave, Milo squealed with excitement.

"This is so much fun!" Milo cried.

The captain turned around and gave us a smile. Noticing the look of terror on my face, he said, "You can sit up here if the waves are bothering you, Birdie. It's not as bumpy and you won't get splashed by the waves as much as you do back there."

"Oh, no thanks. I can't leave my grandson back here alone." I squeezed his hand tighter at the thought of letting go of him.

"Ow, that's a little too tight, Grammy," Milo said, trying to pull his hand away from mine.

"Sorry, but you are my favorite person and I will not let anything happen to you," I said, releasing my grip just a little.

Speed Racer gracefully flew across the water and soon I settled into the rise and fall of the waves, mesmerized by the gentle rocking of our boat. When I finally did relax, I was captivated by the beautiful vast ocean, the smell of the fresh, salty sea air, and the calls of the seagulls overhead. Dark skies loomed in the distance but above us there was blue sky and the bright, shining sun peeked out from behind the clouds.

"Look, I can see the lighthouse!" Milo exclaimed as he suddenly stood up. Instinctively, I grabbed him with my hands and pulled him back down.

"Relax, Grammy," Milo said, rolling his eyes.

I turned to where Milo had pointed but kept one

hand on his shoulder to stop him from getting up again. The fog was thick and heavy, swallowing everything it touched. But when the fog parted like a curtain, I saw a glimpse of the crisp, white lighthouse looming over us. It sat high on top of a steep, rocky cliff. A wide beam of light streaked across the choppy waters filling me with dread as I realized that this was the place we were going to call home for the next month.

"I will take us up to that buoy in the water," the captain called as he slowed the boat down and pointed to a floating red and white buoy. "Even though my boat isn't that big, the shoreline is too rocky for me to safely maneuver us any closer. Once I get the boat anchored, I will hook you up to the zip line, one at a time." It was clear that the fun of the open ocean had passed and now the captain had work to do.

Pulling up to the buoy in the water, the captain swiftly ran to the edge of the boat and tied it up.

Looming overhead was a precariously looking rope. The rope had seen better days and only remnants of its original bright neon green color remained. It stretched from the buoy all the way to the island shore. I stood in shock as I realized I was about to embark upon a very long and perilous trip across the open ocean on a rope that may break at any moment. And worse, I was about to send my beloved grandson into the unknown.

"Alright, we are all set," the captain said, relaxing now that the boat was secure.

"Um, so, what exactly do we do now?" I asked. The waves were picking up as the dark clouds slowly inched closer, ferociously rocking our boat and causing me to feel seasick.

"We need to work quickly because it looks like the rain is going to start any minute." He grabbed a black strap and belt from the boat and started hooking me in.

"Wait, wait, wait. Hold on a minute. Um, what

exactly do I have to do?" Even though I have gone on a lot of adventures in my life, I still sometimes panic when I am about to embark on something new.

"I will hook you up on this end of the rope. Then I will give you a push and you will be off. All you have to do is unhook yourself when you get to the other side. I will send Milo over after you get out of the way. Finally, I will send over the backpacks." The captain showed me how to free myself from the zip line by unclipping the black hook.

I didn't have time to think about what I was about to do because the captain worked with such skill that, before I knew it, I was hooked up to the zip line. I tried to stay calm but I tried even harder to shrug off Milo's giggling.

"Remember, this was your grand idea Grammy," Milo said between laughs.

"Yep, it sure was and I am so excited," I lied. I

did my best to ignore the butterflies zooming through my stomach.

"Alright, you are hooked in. Have a great time and radio me if you need anything," the captain said. Then he gave me a gentle push and I was off.

Screaming with fear and excitement, I flew through the air, my arms and legs thrashing every which way. Water crashed and swirled beneath me, waves occasionally splashing up and pelting me with their force. The wind was howling so loudly that I could barely hear my own screaming. It was the most exhilarating experience of my life, though I wouldn't admit that until my feet were safely back on the ground.

It was over before I had time to fully register what had happened. I ungracefully and awkwardly crashed into the end of the zip line. As fast as I could with my trembling hands, I unclipped myself and collapsed with a thud on the sand, relieved to be back on sturdy ground.

However, my relief was short lived as I realized it was now Milo's turn. I could just barely make out his dark figure dangling from the zip line far out in the roaring ocean. The rain beat down from the black sky and the wind howled louder than I had ever heard before. It sounded like a monstrous roar as it echoed off the sea caves surrounding the island. Horrified, I watched as the ocean transformed into mountains of furious waves ready to devour anyone foolish enough to enter.

Milo gave me a thumbs up, the captain gave him a push, and he was off. He sailed through the storm with grace and ease, looking as though he had done this at least one hundred times before. Even though it was dark and pouring rain, Milo never stopped smiling. He gently placed his feet on the ground and landed quietly.

"That was awesome!" Milo exclaimed as I helped unhook him from the zip line. "When can we do it again?"

...y, very long time," I

...rack of lightening.

The captain clipped our backpacks to the zip line and sent them over with a big push. They looked creepy flying through the storm by themselves, resembling a pair of ghosts preparing to attack an intruder.

"Our backpacks are more graceful than you on the zip line," Milo laughed.

"Yeah, I have to admit that I agree with you on that one," I said. The hook was wet and slippery and I wasn't sure if I was going to be able to free our backpacks from the zip line. My frustration grew, matching the fierceness of the storm, with each failed attempt to release them. I was about to give up and admit defeat when I heard a click and they landed on the wet sand with a bang.

As soon as I succeeded, the captain sprang into action, quickly untying the boat from the buoy. He waved goodbye as he sped off into the storm. The

thick fog immediately swallowed Speed Racer,
leaving us completely and utterly alone.

Chapter 3

The growling thunderstorm lit up the sky with unrelenting force while my mind whirled with thoughts of how alone and far away we were from the world I thought I knew so well. I have lived through many thunderstorms, but never one as ferocious as this. "We need to get to the lighthouse before this storm eats us alive!" I yelled. I grabbed my backpack and slung it over my shoulders then paused as I considered what to do with Milo's.

Suddenly, the waves crashed against the shore with such force that they ripped a tree from its roots before sucking it like prey into the ocean.

"Let's get out of here! Now!" Milo screamed, his voice barely audible over the roar of the storm.

Without another thought, I heaved Milo's backpack on to my back. Then I looked up at the looming cliffs that towered high above us. Unfortunately, the only way to the lighthouse was to go up. The rocks jutted out in a formation that resembled a medieval staircase.

"Too bad there isn't an elevator on the island," Milo said as he grasped hold of a rocky edge and stepped onto the first stone. He skillfully maneuvered his way up the cliffs, occasionally pausing to look back at me. I followed as closely as I could. The rocks were slippery, slimy, and full of moss. The added weight from our backpacks slowed me down. But eventually, I made it.

Milo ducked under a rocky overhang, getting some relief from the unrelenting rain while patiently waiting for me. "To the lighthouse," he proclaimed as soon as I caught up with him. He bounded ahead and disappeared into the fog.

A tight grip of panic took hold of me the moment Milo disappeared. Even though I was out of breath from the climb, I ran as fast as I could to try and find him. Eventually I saw the mysterious lighthouse through the fog but I still could not find Milo.

The flickering orange beam of light from the lighthouse pierced the darkness, revealing ghostly shadows everywhere I looked. My panic turned to despair as I searched in vain for my beloved grandson. "Milo!!! Where are you!?!?" I screamed.

"Um, right next to you." Milo was standing only a few feet from me but because of the fog he remained hidden.

"Oh, sorry. I didn't see you there." I tried to catch my breath as I felt my heartbeat slowing down. "Come on, let's go inside."

"No way! I am not going in there!" Milo pointed a shaking finger at the lighthouse. "What if there is a ghost inside? Maybe Lady Gray came back to haunt the place? Maybe there are pirates? Or witches?" Milo looked out at the crashing waves, clearly contemplating a possible escape route.

"I think if there is anything inside, it will be a mouse or possibly a bat. Ghosts aren't real!" I bravely turned the old brass door handle and the door slowly creaked open.

I stepped into the kitchen but it felt like I had stepped back in time. The kitchen stove was hundreds of years old. It was black with silver doors and brass handles. On top of the stove was an old cast iron tea kettle which had probably been used thousands of times over the years. The old wood table was surrounded by a set of four ornately carved wood chairs. The chairs resembled trees with long branches hanging down. A lantern sat in the center of the table.

Milo cautiously peeked into the kitchen. "Hello! Is anyone here?"

The only response was the howling wind as it echoed through the lighthouse. "How do you turn the lights on?" He fumbled around, searching the walls for a light switch. Even though it was still daytime, because of the storm, it was pitch dark inside.

"You won't find a light switch, Milo." I put our wet backpacks on the floor and shut the door. It slammed noisily with a bang, causing the tea kettle to rattle and Milo to jump and spin around.

"Oops, I must have pushed the door too hard. Sorry," I said.

"What do you mean I won't find a light switch? There has to be one here somewhere," Milo said. He bumped into the table as he tried to make his way to the other side of the dark room.

"There isn't any electricity on the island. We have to use lanterns." I pointed to the lantern on the table.

Milo grabbed the lantern and inspected it. "It is

heavier than I thought it would be. Where's the switch on this thing?" he asked as he turned it over to look on the bottom.

"It's a gas lantern. I will have to light it." Luckily I found a set of matches without too much trouble. I held a match to the wick and instantly a dim light illuminated the room with a flickering yellow glow.

"Well, that's better!" Milo said. He looked around the historic kitchen in awe. "Um, Grammy? I have to go the bathroom."

"I will take you out to it."

"Take me out to it?"

"Did I forget to mention that there isn't any plumbing on the island? But, don't worry because there is a very nice outhouse nearby," I said, trying to sound excited about our bathroom accommodations.

"An outhouse? There isn't a bathroom inside the lighthouse? I think you forgot to mention that to me on purpose, Grammy!"

"Me? Do something like that? Never!" I said with a sly smile. "Come on, let's go find it. It can't be that bad."

I opened the front door and scanned the yard, searching for our bathroom. About one hundred feet away, tucked into some trees sat a rickety, old wood structure. The roof sagged in spots and it was surrounded by overgrown grass that inched its way up the sides of the outhouse. The strong winds had forced open the door. The entrance looked like a black hole leading to an underworld that nobody ever returned from.

"Oh, look! It's right over there," I said, trying to sound cheerful. "Nice and close by! That will be great for me when I have to use it in the middle of the night." It was getting harder and harder to hide my despair over having to use an outhouse for a month as my bathroom.

"That thing looks like it's going to cave in any minute!" Milo exclaimed.

"If Lady Gray could do this for fifty years, then I think we can do it for one month," I said.

The rain temporarily slowed and Milo said, "I would rather pee on the bushes. Nobody is around, right?"

"No, it is just us. But, I think we can attempt to maintain some sort of civility while living on the island, can't we Milo?"

"You can but I'm going to live on the wild side," Milo exclaimed as he jumped off the stairs into the grass and raced for a nearby bush. I turned away to give him some privacy, though I doubt that he cared.

Moments later Milo bounded back up the stairs and into the kitchen. "That was great! May I run around in my underwear ..."

"No, Milo!" I quickly changed the subject. "Let's make dinner and start the puzzle you brought. Tomorrow when the sun returns we will explore the lighthouse."

"What's for dinner?" Milo asked. With wide eyes, he suspiciously looked at the old stove. "And, where's the food?"

"I don't know. But I am sure the Park Patrol wouldn't leave us without food." I opened up the first cupboard door. It was empty. I opened up the second cupboard door. It was empty. I opened up the third door and of course found it empty. Panicking, I scrambled around the kitchen, opening and closing every single door. I found some plates, bowls, cups, and silverware. Unfortunately, they would not be of much use because I did not find any food.

I was starving and my stomach would not stop grumbling. "I wonder where the radio is." I searched the walls for something that resembled a telephone. "I will call the captain and politely beg him to bring us some food. A thick crust cheese pizza sounds great!"

Milo looked at me like I was crazy. "I don't think

he is going to bring us a pizza. Besides, I don't know if we want him coming back. He said he's not a pirate but you never know. Maybe after dark, he turns into one and he doesn't even know it. He likes to go on overnight trips to deserted islands. He is probably doing all sorts of secret pirate stuff in the middle of the night!"

Milo pulled on the seat of a long wooden bench that stretched across the length of the wall next to the front door. Surprisingly it opened, revealing a hidden chamber within the bench. The inside was lined with air tight coolers. "Look!" he cried. "I think I found the food."

The coolers were packed with supplies. Noodles, spaghetti sauce, canned beans, oatmeal, and rice were all stacked neatly in the coolers. On top of the last cooler was an envelope. "What's this, Grammy?" Milo asked as he handed it to me.

I opened the envelope and scanned the letter. "So, what does it say, Grammy?" Milo asked, searching my face for clues. "Is it good news? Do they have pizza delivery?"

"Unfortunately it does not say anything about pizza delivery. Apparently there is a bit of a mouse problem in the lighthouse. That is why the Park Patrol put the food inside the coolers. It also says that there is a vegetable garden on the island. They would like us to take care of it and we are welcome to eat whatever we want from it."

"That sounds fun!" Milo exclaimed. "Do you know how to garden?"

"Um … no … not really. I have a few house plants. Though I have replaced them from time to time after they died. Once I kept a plant alive for almost an entire year!"

"Why is this not surprising," Milo said, shaking his head. "So, I guess we can't have pizza for dinner?"

"No, we definitely can't have pizza for dinner." I rummaged through the food and finally settled on the spaghetti noodles and tomato sauce. "This should be easy to make and I know you like spaghetti."

"Yum!" Milo exclaimed. He dug out the puzzle from his backpack and sat down at the kitchen table. He watched me for a while as I tried to maneuver my way through the unfamiliar kitchen. Finally, becoming bored, he took the top of the puzzle box off and began sorting out the edge pieces.

After searching through the cupboards, I sat down at the table with him, exhausted and frustrated. "I can't find a cooking pot anywhere! I've never eaten raw noodles before but there's a first time for everything!"

"It's right there, Grammy," Milo calmly said without taking his eyes off the puzzle and pointing to a pot hanging on the wall.

"I never thought to look there!" I said with relief. I took it down from the wall and peered inside the empty pot. "Now, how do I fill this with water?"

"There is a well outside," Milo said.

"A well?"

"Yes, I saw a bucket attached to a long rope."

"Hmmm. A well and a bucket."

"Yep, a well and a bucket," Milo said, amused.

"This will be fun. I will be right back," I said with as much confidence as I could muster.

"Don't forget your raincoat. It's pouring again," Milo said.

I put on my dripping wet raincoat and opened the front door. Scanning the yard, I spotted a circular stone well roughly twenty yards from the lighthouse door. I dashed through the yard as fast as I could but the pouring rain soaked me instantly.

A brown rope hung from a pulley and a bucket was clipped to the end. I grabbed hold of the slippery, wet rope and pulled it through my hands. The bucket sank deeper and deeper into the well until it disappeared into darkness. It was much heavier and harder to do than I expected. It took a few minutes of pulling but finally the bucket reappeared. To my surprise and delight, it was full of water.

I unhooked the bucket and raced for the lighthouse. Milo stood at the front door, intently watching me. As I ran, the water splashed out of the bucket and spilled on the ground.

"You might have to go back for more. I think you spilled most of it!"

"We don't need that much water for spaghetti," I said.

I put the water bucket down on the kitchen floor and took off my rain coat. "Now I just need to figure out how to light the burner on the stove."

"I don't think I am going to need this puzzle after all. Watching you is so much more entertaining!" Milo chuckled.

I examined the stove for much longer than necessary, unsure of what to do. After I silently gave myself a pep talk, I grabbed the matches and prepared to light it. "I don't have a gas stove at home, but it looks like all I have to do is flip the switch and hold a burning match to it."

"Are you going to burn this place down, Grammy?" Milo asked.

"I don't think so." Seeing the concerned look on Milo's face, I corrected myself. "I mean, no! Of course not!" Before he or I could give this anymore thought, I flipped the switch, lit the match, and held it up to where the gas seemed to be coming out. A moment later, there was a crackle and a flame sprang up, filling the stove with warmth.

"Ah ha! I knew I could do it!"

Milo filled the cooking pot with the well water and handed it to me. I placed it on the stove and opened up the jar of sauce. It did not take long for the old stove to heat up our water. Soon the kitchen was filled with warmth and delicious smells from our spaghetti dinner. We filled our bowls with spaghetti and sat down to eat. We silently and cheerfully devoured all of the food.

I used the rest of the well water to wash the dishes and then Milo and I stayed up late working on the puzzle. We only got about a quarter of the edge pieces put together before we decided to go to bed.

"Where are the beds, Grammy?" Milo asked as we left the kitchen and darkness fell upon us.

"Probably upstairs," I said as we approached a steep, dark staircase.

Terrified, Milo said, "I'm not going up there in the dark. No way! You can't make me!"

It was clear that it was not going to be easy to convince Milo to go upstairs and I didn't really want to explore in the dark either, so I agreed. "For tonight, let's just sleep down here."

"Fine with me!" Milo said, relieved.

We were happy to find a wood burning fireplace, comfy chairs, and a couch in what we would call our living room for the next month. There was a pile of warm, cozy blankets draped over the edge of the couch. Milo jumped onto it and stretched out. Because the couch was short, he took up the entire length.

"I will take the chair." I tucked him in as best I could and gave him a kiss goodnight. Exhausted, I plopped down into the chair and almost instantly fell asleep.

Chapter 4

"Grammy, are you awake?" Milo whispered. "Did you hear that?"

I did not respond so he tried again. This time, much louder. "GRAMMY!!"

I flew out of my chair and the blankets tumbled to the ground. Terrified, I spun around in circles, ready to pounce. "What's wrong, Milo?"

"We aren't alone, Grammy!" Milo pulled his blanket tightly over his head. All that stuck out were a few strands of his light brown hair.

It was the middle of the night and the room was

completely dark. I shivered from the cold, damp air. I picked up my blankets from the ground and wrapped one around my shoulders. "We aren't alone?"

"No, we are not! Somebody or something lives in this creepy, old lighthouse," Milo said, still hiding under his blankets.

"You are right about that. We live here. At least for a little while," I said, yawning.

"Not us! Somebody else is here! I heard footsteps and I think they were coming from the kitchen."

"Stay here. I will go investigate." Milo didn't move. If anyone else was here, they would be terrified of what looked like a mummy under the blanket on the couch.

I lit the lantern and silently made my way to the kitchen. The spooky yellow glow illuminated the kitchen table where Milo and I had eaten our spaghetti only hours earlier. Everything looked exactly as I had left it.

"There is nothing here," I said loud enough for Milo to hear.

Suddenly I heard tiny, scrambling footsteps behind me. I spun around, ready to face our intruders. "EEEK!" I shrieked as I ran into the living room. In my haste, I grabbed a corn husk broom that was resting against the wall in the hallway.

"Should I run for my life?" Milo said, trembling under his blankets.

I flew into the room and jumped onto my chair. I stood on top of it and wildly waved the broom around in the air.

"Depending on how you feel about mice, you may or may not need to run for your life!" I put the lantern on a table and slowly sat down, making sure to keep my feet off the ground.

"Mice?" Milo asked, peeking his head out from under his blanket.

"Yep. It turns out that those intruders you were worried about are actually mice. Harmless little mice."

"If they are so harmless than why are you waving that broom around like a sword? And why are your feet up in the air?"

"Make fun of me all you want. But I cannot stand having mice in my house. I really, really, really do not like them! We should have brought a cat with us."

"A cat? What for?" Milo asked, surprised.

"Because the cat would eat the mice," I said.

"That's terrible, Grammy. Why would you want a cat to hurt those poor, little creatures?"

"It's not that I want the cat to hurt them but I refuse to live with mice."

"But you are willing to live with a cat. That's a creature, too."

"Yes, that's true. However biased it may seem, I do prefer some creatures over others."

"Grammy, you of all people should be treating all things equally. You are the one who taught me to be kind to all living things. Are you telling me that mice are an exception?"

"It's silly, I know. I just don't like them." I put one toe on the floor and tried to look brave.

"Tomorrow I will work on catching them and putting them outside," Milo said.

"Thanks! That would be great! In the meantime, I will keep watch and make sure the killer mice do not attack us."

I looked at my watch. It was three o'clock in the morning. Milo soon fell back asleep but I just couldn't relax. With every creak and moan, I found myself standing on top of my chair expecting a group of attack mice to come and eat me. Of course, they never did come.

I felt quite foolish when the sun started to peek up from the horizon and I was still on the lookout. Milo was sound asleep so I quietly made myself a cup of coffee and took it outside. I found a set of lawn chairs near the cliff edge, overlooking the beautiful blue ocean.

The world I knew so well back home was nothing like the world I was experiencing here. There were no other sounds except for the quiet lapping of the waves against the shoreline and the joyful singing of the birds as they welcomed a new day.

As the sky was turning a brilliant shade of orange, Milo came out to greet me. "I see you made it through the night alive, Grammy."

"Please excuse my behavior last night. Apparently I never told you that I have an irrational fear of mice. It started when I was a child not much older than you. I was getting ready to go for a hike. I had my shoes on, snacks packed, and my water bottle ready to go. Finally, I picked up my backpack. Out of nowhere, a mouse jumped out of it and landed on my foot! Ever since then, I have been terrified of mice. Not just terrified. Horrified, shocked, and scared out of my mind." I gritted my teeth at the memory of the mouse running across my foot.

"If you don't face your fears, you will never conquer them," Milo said. "So today, together, we are going to try to catch the mice."

"I thought you could do that while I ..."

Interrupting, Milo put his hand on my shoulder. "You can do this, Grammy. I know you can do this."

Looking into his hopeful, brown eyes, I couldn't bring myself to let Milo down. "Okay, you are right. Today is the day I conquer my fear of mice!"

After a quick breakfast of oatmeal and berries, we started our mice catching operation. Milo found a box and placed a cracker inside. Then he attached a string to the lid and propped it open. "If a mouse runs in, the string will unhook and the lid will close, trapping the mouse inside. Then you will carry the box outside and let the mouse run free!"

"Um … actually, I think it is better if you carry the box outside," I said, biting my lip.

"Nope, you are going to do it!"

"Please don't let us catch a mouse. Please, please, please don't let us catch a mouse," I mumbled to myself as I washed our breakfast dishes.

"You know I can hear you, right?" Milo said. He put the box of oatmeal into the cooler inside the bench. As he closed it, he suddenly yelled, "Look out! A mouse!"

Terrified, I dropped a spoon on the floor and spun around ready to run for my life.

Milo keeled over with laughter. "Oh Grammy, it is so much fun to trick you! You should have seen the look on your face! You do know that the mice are more afraid of you than you are of them."

"Not funny, Milo!" As I reached down to pick up the spoon, I noticed a trap door in the floor under the kitchen table. I quickly got down on my hands and knees and crawled over to it.

"You are not going to find a mouse that way, Grammy," Milo said. His curiosity got the best of him and he was soon next to me on all fours. He immediately noticed the door. "What's that?"

"It looks like a door," I said.

"A secret door! Cool! I bet this place has hidden treasure!" Milo exclaimed. He pulled on the black handle. The sound of the creaking door brought chills to my spine. Intricately built spider webs dangled across the opening. The strands were so thick that we could not see what was behind them.

Moving closer, I instinctively pulled the spider webs to the side. The sticky strands tore apart and got stuck to my hands. Though some of the web remained in place, we could see through the silken strands that waved mysteriously in the air. A rickety, wood staircase disappeared into darkness.

"Do you think we should investigate? What if we find ghosts and monsters down there? Maybe it would be better to just close the door and pretend it is not there? Then again, we might find treasure," Milo said. He was scared and excited at the same time.

"I think we have an obligation to investigate. We are caretakers of the island and the lighthouse, so I think part of our job is to know our way around this place. Let's grab some lanterns and go exploring!" I said.

Chapter 5

"Beverly!" Fable bellowed. He sat reclined in his chair with his bare feet propped up on his desk while munching on cheese puffs.

Beverly froze, terrified that Fable knew she was reading a book instead of doing the work he had assigned her for the day. Thinking quickly, she pushed her book under a legal pad and ran to his office.

"Yes," Beverly said, giving Fable an innocent smile. Behind her back she crossed her fingers, hoping Fable had not picked up on her reading habits at work.

Fable Finch is an attorney in Greenville. However, he is not the most popular attorney in town. In fact, he is the least liked attorney for miles around. People discovered over the years that Fable is greedy … very, very greedy. He only cares about money and making more money. He will stop at nothing to make money and gladly steps on anyone who gets in his way.

Beverly is Fable's trusted assistant and has been putting up with him and his obnoxious behavior for years simply because she rarely has any work to do. Fable has had very few clients over the years. This leaves Beverly free to spend her time pretending she is hard at work when most of the time she is reading a good book.

"Did you see this announcement in the newspaper?" Fable said with a mischievous smirk.

"Which announcement is that, Fable?" Beverly asked.

"This one, right here," Fable answered, pointing at the paper and waving it in the air. "This is so exciting! Some crazy person has offered a $100 reward for anyone who can find out why the Greenville River is drying up! This is our lucky day … or my lucky day because I, and when I say I, I actually mean you, are going to solve this mystery so I can get paid!"

"How exactly am I supposed to figure that out?" Beverly asked. She pulled up the blinds, letting in a stream of warm, golden sunlight.

"You are going to take a chair and sit at the end of the river to see who is taking the water. It will be a very simple project and I am confident you will figure this out for me."

"Sit at the end of the river?" Beverly asked, confused.

"Yes, sit. You are lucky I am permitting you to take a chair. I could have said you have to go stand there until you figure it out. But do not take any of my good chairs. I think there is an old beach chair in one of the closets. As soon as you find it, you are released to go start your assignment," Fable said.

He closed the blinds that Beverly had just opened. "I like it dark in here. Plus, people tend to stare at me when they walk by. Probably because I am such a celebrity around town."

With a sigh, Beverly turned to leave the office. "I will give you $2 out of the $100 after your successful completion of this crucial assignment. You are such a great asset to my incredible law practice. Get on out there Beverly! I know you can do it!"

It took Beverly an hour to find the old beach chair. It was wedged all the way in the back of a closet that was stuffed full of newly acquired snacks. She grabbed a few bags of crackers and secretly tucked them into her purse. Luckily she had a stash of her favorite books hidden in her desk drawer, so she chose a few and stuffed them in next to her snacks. She picked up her sunglasses, put on her sweater, and left the office without saying goodbye to Fable.

Beverly drove to the Greenville River and followed the road that ran alongside it. The green old-growth forest immediately put her at ease and she could feel her annoyance with Fable disappearing. She rolled down her windows. The fresh, clean country air swirled through the car and the sounds of the birds delighted her. The thick, dense forest was full of life.

It was hard to keep her eyes on the road. Beverly found herself glancing at the river as it twisted and looped its way around the forest, looking like it would never end. Suddenly, she slammed her breaks as she abruptly and unexpectedly came upon the end of the river.

Beverly parked her car on the edge of the road. It was eerily silent as she stepped outside. What moments ago was a wondrous, mighty river was now completely gone. Dead fish, turtles and frogs littered the ground. It smelled awful, even worse than Fable's office.

She grabbed her purse from the front seat and yanked the chair out from the trunk of her car. Then she waded through the tall, brown grass that led to the muddy riverbed. She set up her chair under an ancient, gnarled tree in order to get some protection from the sun.

She plopped down in her chair and looked around. There wasn't another human being in sight. Except for an occasional turkey vulture or hawk flying overhead, Beverly was completely and utterly alone. At first this scared her, but after a few moments she relaxed and felt at ease.

"This is going to be a long day," she said to herself as she pulled out her favorite book and a bag of crackers. Just as she was opening up her book to the first page, a car unexpectedly raced around a bend in the road and squealed to a stop.

Beverly groaned as soon as she realized it was Fable. Leaving his car running, he got out from the driver's seat. "I am here to check in and make sure you are hard at work!" he declared.

"Yep, that's me! Always hard at work for you," Beverly said, sheepishly. She skillfully slipped her book under her so Fable would not see it.

"I forgot to tell you to take a pad of paper and pen so you can record the evidence you find," Fable said. He handed her a chewed up pen and a pad of paper that was covered in stains. It looked as though someone (probably him) had spilled coffee all over it. "You know, you will solve this mystery faster if you get up and investigate. You have to think like a detective not a legal assistant."

"I am just settling in," Beverly said, annoyed. "I am sure I will try out many different mystery solving tactics soon."

"Always doing your best, that's what I like about you," Fable said as he turned to leave. He gave her a thumbs up as he sped off around the bend, leaving Beverly once again in silence.

Chapter 6

Milo and I peered down the precarious, steep staircase, frozen in place with fear of the unknown.

"Maybe we should just close the door and pretend there is nothing here," Milo suggested.

"We can ignore reality but we cannot change reality." I put my foot onto the first stair. "My curiosity is not going to allow me to let this go. And I bet yours will not either." The stair creaked and groaned under my weight, sounding as though it may collapse at any moment, causing me to tumble into the dark abyss.

"Before I go any further, please hand me the

broom. Just in in case we encounter any killer mice."

"If the only thing we run into is a mouse, than we should consider ourselves lucky," Milo said as he handed it to me.

"Maybe so," I whispered. I ducked down to avoid hitting my head on the low stone ceiling as I descended into darkness. The air was thick with dust, making my nose itch. I suddenly stopped, causing Milo to run into me. "Shoo! Get out of here! Judge Birdie is here and you need to get out of my way!!!!!"

"Do you see something?" Milo asked, terrified.

"No. I am just making sure that the mice know we are here so that they run away and hide before we get down there," I said, pointing into the darkness.

"Hey, mice! Judge Birdie's bed is super warm and cozy and it isn't being used right now!" Milo shouted.

"Not funny, Milo. Not funny." I tried to glare at him, but my smile deceived me.

As we continued down the stairs we unexpectedly came upon a portrait of a young girl hanging on the wall. She was dressed all in white. In her hands she clutched a pirate ship. Her eyes were icy blue and her gaze followed us as we moved past her. Her pink lips were pursed together in a tight frown. Immediately I was reminded of the ghost story from *Beware of Ghost Island* about a girl in white floating around the top of the lighthouse. I tried to force the terrifying story from my mind.

"I think that girl is looking at us," Milo whispered.

I reached up to touch the painting, hoping to prove that it was truly only a painting. I ran my fingers over the smooth surface. It felt much colder than the air around us and I suddenly shivered. Her icy, blue eyes looked deep into my own, filling me with a feeling of dread.

I pulled my hand away and the cold instantly receded. "Come on, Milo. Let's keep going." Forgetting about being cautious, I bounded down the stairs and away from the creepy portrait as fast as my feet could take me.

It seemed to take forever, but we finally reached the bottom. The air was cool, musty and damp, causing me to shiver with a sudden chill. Giant spider webs hung in every corner, all of which were overflowing with their victims. "Looks like the spiders are well fed," I joked, trying to lighten the mood.

"That web is so huge, I bet it could trap me!" Milo pointed at an enormous spider web. It stretched in circles covering an entire corner of the room, reaching from floor to ceiling.

"Well, at least they are helping keep the bug population in check for us! Did you know that spiders eat more insects than birds and bats, combined?"

"I hope they don't eat people," Milo said, still frozen in place on the last stair, ready to turn and run if necessary.

"I don't think we have to worry about that. Lady Gray lived here for fifty years without a problem."

"Maybe a killer spider ate her," Milo yelped, turning to go back upstairs.

"We don't live in the tropics, Milo. I really don't think we need to worry about poisonous spiders."

"What do you think this place is?" Milo asked, turning back around.

Rickety wood shelves lined the stone walls, old barrels covered the circumference of the room, and a small table full of crates sat in a far corner.

"This is a root cellar!" I exclaimed with delight as I peered into an old barrel. "Lady Gray has been busy! The barrels are full of potatoes, onions, and winter squash. And look at this!" I picked up a jar from a shelf and held it up for Milo to see.

"What's that? Eyeballs?" Milo cried.

"No, not eyeballs!" I laughed. "These are pickled onions! And here are some pickled green beans, and pickled beets, and pickled asparagus! And look, your favorite, dill pickles!" I handed Milo a glass jar full of dill pickles. The green spears were packed tightly in the jar. Sprigs of dill and chunks of garlic floated around in the vinegar.

"Do you think they are safe to eat?" Milo asked, inspecting the jar.

"The lids are tightly sealed," I said as I pushed my thumb onto the top of the jar. "See, the lid did not pop. That means it is sealed. Oh, and look! Lady Gray wrote the canning year on the bottom of each jar. This is excellent. Now there is no way we will starve!"

"I didn't know starving was an option." Milo picked up a jar containing a thick, viscous, red liquid. He gave it a gentle shake and watched it swirl around, forming a tornado. "Is this blood?"

"Tomato juice! Just think of all the good food

we can make!"

"I will let you try it first, just in case it is blood. Or worse, poison!" He put the jar of tomatoes back on the shelf before inspecting the contents of the other jars. "I wonder what this is?" Milo pushed a row of glass jars to the side and reached to the back of the shelf. He carefully pulled out a wooden box that looked to be hundreds of years old. He blew on the top, sending a plume of dust flying up into the air. He tugged at the clasp but it didn't budge. "It's locked!"

I took the box from Milo and turned it around, inspecting it. The ornate carvings resembled a pirate ship looming on the ocean, cannons at the ready. A mermaid sat upon a rock. Strangely, the pirate ship looked exactly like the one the girl was holding in the painting. "It's beautiful! I wonder if we can find the key?"

We searched every nook and cranny of the root cellar, avoiding the spider webs as best we could.

Just as we were about to give up, Milo tipped a barrel onto its side, peering underneath. "I think I found it!" he exclaimed.

I held up the barrel while Milo reached under. Moments later he emerged with a brass key. Running over to the box, Milo put the key into the lock and turned. The lock clicked and the door popped open.

"Oh man! This is so exciting!" Milo cried. He opened the lid and discovered a tattered, tightly rolled scroll. The edges were crinkled and brown with age. It was tied closed with a metallic, gold string. "I think we just found a treasure map!"

"Let's take it upstairs so we can look it over in the daylight. Plus, I am ready to get some fresh air," I said with a sneeze. Because we had disturbed the barrels and jars, the air was now thick and heavy with dust. I carefully closed the lid and took the box from Milo. "Grab a jar of pickles and a few potatoes. We can eat them for lunch." I excitedly grabbed a jar of pickled mushrooms (my favorite) and some onions before nestling them into the crook of my arm.

Milo filled his arms with as much as he could carry and we slowly made our way back up the rickety, steep stairs. I only glanced at the girl in the painting once. This time, it looked like her lips were upturned in a menacing smile and her eyes glowed with fury.

The bright light of the day blinded us as we stepped back into the kitchen. I quickly slammed the trap door closed and latched it. With any luck, that will keep the young girl down there, I thought to myself as I pushed the table over the secret door. "I don't believe in ghosts," I reminded myself, shaking my head with disbelief.

I put the box on the table, opened the lid, and took out the scroll. A spider jumped off the box and scurried away, hiding itself within the cracks of the kitchen floor.

"Do you think it's a treasure map?" Milo asked. Unable to stand still, he hopped up and down with excitement.

"I don't know." I untied the gold string and unrolled the scroll. "I can't believe this!" With trembling hands, I laid the scroll on top of the table, holding onto the edges so it would not roll up again. The air smelled musty from centuries-old paper. A detailed map of the island was drawn on the scroll in black marker. A path led to a beach where there was a big red X written in red marker. On the bottom corner of the map were the initials *£.G.* written in thick cursive letters.

"Treasure!" Milo proclaimed.

Chapter 7

Beverly watched as the dirt disturbed by Mr. Finch's car slowly settled back down to the ground. Again left alone with her thoughts, she sat in her chair listening to the birds and watching the wind rustle the leaves of the trees. She soon became bored and decided to go for a walk in the woods.

She wound her way down the old dirt road until she encountered an overgrown trail. "Maybe this is a deer trail," she thought as she headed into the woods. The golden sunlight streamed down through the trees, illuminating the different shades of greens. "This must be heaven on earth," she said to herself as she admired the beauty that surrounded her.

Beverly found herself taking deep breaths of the fresh, humid air as she maneuvered through the brambles that had begun their quest to take over as much of the forest as they could. As she stepped over a particularly large patch of brambles, she noticed that they were not just a nuisance of thorny bushes to be avoided. She was delighted to discover that they were loaded with fresh black raspberries! Overjoyed, she stopped for a delicious snack.

It did not take long before her fingers were stained a deep, rich purple. After she had her fill, she continued on the path, stepping over fallen tree branches and inspecting rocks that had unearthed themselves at the base of the trees.

Before long, she came upon a fallen elm tree. Bending down to inspect the root ball that left the earth broken and exposed, she noticed a group of mushrooms. They were medium-sized, cone-shaped and light brown. "If it wasn't for their brown color, I would think this might be honeycomb," she thought as she towered over them.

"I think these might be morel mushrooms! People in town are always ranting and raving about them." She plucked them out of the ground, shaped the bottom of her shirt into a basket, and piled them in. "I better take these with me, just in case they are morels. I've always wanted to try one, but they are too expensive for me."

Beverly kept going on the path until she came to a clear, sparkling brook. Pausing to take a break, she found a rock on the edge of the water and sat down. She took off her shoes and stuck her toes into the shallow water. Closing her eyes, she listened to the sounds of the rushing water and felt it running through her toes. "This is so much better than working in the office."

Unhurriedly, Beverly made her way back to her car. She found an empty bag in her trunk and carefully put the mushrooms inside before lying it on the front seat. The sun was low in the sky so she decided to pack up her chair and head home for the day. She felt a pain in her heart as she drove away from the beautiful, quiet countryside knowing she was headed back to the hustle and bustle of city life.

After she arrived home, she promptly headed to her computer to look up information about morel mushrooms. After she confirmed that she had in fact found a gold mine, she skipped to the kitchen to prepare her delicacies.

Beverly gently shook off as much dirt as she could before rinsing the mushrooms under cool water. She laid them out on a towel and put a pat of butter in her cast iron skillet. The smell of melting butter made her stomach growl and she realized she had not eaten anything since her snack of fresh berries back in the forest. Just the thought of that moment in her life made her smile.

Beverly thinly sliced the mushrooms and fried

them for a few minutes in the butter. When they were done, she sprinkled them with salt and piled them onto her plate.

"Aren't I fancy now," she said to herself as she made her way to her formal dining room table. The mushrooms smelled really good but they tasted even better. She slowly ate them, closing her eyes and savoring every single bite, knowing that she may never be so lucky as to find morels again.

After dinner, Beverly made herself a cup of chamomile tea and went out to her porch swing. She found herself daydreaming about changing careers. Particularly any job where she could work outside and, more importantly, far away from that greedy Mr. Finch.

"Forest ranger, botanist, marine biologist, paleontologist, wildlife biologist, archaeologist, geoscientist. The possibilities are endless! Yes, I think it is time for a career change," Beverly mused.

After she finished her cup of tea, she headed for

bed. That night she dreamt she was studying bats in a tropical rainforest. It was the greatest night sleep of her entire life! When she awoke in the morning, she was certain that her old life was gone and that she was about to embark on a new and exciting adventure!

Chapter 8

"I thought we might find ghosts and monsters on the island but I never thought we would find treasure!" Milo squealed with delight.

"Yeah, ghosts and monsters are totally more likely," I laughed. I stared at the crinkled, yellow paper, my body covered with goosebumps.

"We have to follow it and figure out what is at the end of this map. It has us going through the woods, into a ravine, up some hills and to a beach. Come on, Grammy! Let's go!" Milo grabbed my hand and tried to pull me out the front door.

"Hold on. I want to go but I think we need to

explore the lighthouse first. I really don't want to sleep on a chair again. Let's see if we can find a bed. Plus, we haven't gone up to the top of the lighthouse yet."

Milo looked sad, so I added, "We are going to need a full day to go treasure hunting. I don't think we should be out after dark. Tomorrow morning, we will get up and leave as soon as it is light out. That should give us plenty of time to find the treasure and get home before dark."

"Alright," Milo grumbled, disappointed that we were not starting our treasure hunt immediately. "I definitely don't want to be out there in the dark." He pointed toward the rocky cliffs and shrugged his shoulders. Without another word, Milo raced out of the kitchen and disappeared into the unexplored lighthouse, apparently already moving on to new adventures.

We found an office next to the kitchen. Though it was small, it had enough room to fit a desk and two bookshelves full of dusty books. The window looked out upon the surrounding forest. On top of the desk Milo found a journal and pen, possibly left behind by Lady Gray.

"Look, Grammy!" Milo fearfully exclaimed as he pointed to the first page of the journal. I stepped closer for a better look.

> The dreadful noises kept me up all night! I didn't get a wink of sleep!

"That could mean anything," I said, doing my best to sound bored. "Maybe there was a thunderstorm, or it was windy, or maybe …"

"This place is haunted!" Milo yelled, terrified.

"No it is not. Ghosts are not real. They are made up creatures by creative imaginations. Some people love a good scare!"

"Not me," Milo said, grabbing my hand.

We spent the next few hours exploring the lighthouse. The rooms were filled with antique furniture, books, and lanterns. The walls were covered in old pictures. A large mirror hung on the wall above the couch.

A narrow, winding staircase led upstairs where we found three bedrooms. The beds were surprisingly soft and comfortable. They were piled high with fuzzy, fleece blankets. Evidently, Lady Gray liked to stay warm. We were thrilled to discover a few board games tucked under one of the beds.

"How do you get to the top of the lighthouse?" Milo asked.

Before I could answer him, a loud bang from a door slamming downstairs made us jump so high we almost hit our heads on the ceiling.

"AAAAHHHH!" Milo screamed. He raced across the room and stood behind me, trying to hide. "I bet it is the ghost from the painting! She saw us take the treasure map and she is trying to scare us out of here before we find the treasure!"

"I am pretty sure that painting was just a really

good painting," I said, trying my best to hide the fear in my voice. I could not stop thinking about the eerie look in the girl's eyes and my mind was starting to believe that there might actually be a ghost living with us. "Come on, let's go investigate." I needed to confirm that the girl from the painting was not floating around the kitchen.

Milo was too afraid to stay upstairs alone, so he was left with no other choice but to follow me.

As we tiptoed into the living room, Milo shrieked, "The rocking chair is rocking!"

Strangely, though it sat empty, the rocking chair in the corner of the room was mysteriously rocking all by itself. "Maybe the mice did it?" I joked.

"We are going to disappear just like Lady Gray did!" Milo cried.

Terrified, I watched the haunted rocking chair slowly rock back and forth, back and forth.

Being the adult, I felt it was my place to reassure Milo and put him at ease, even though I was terrified. "There has to be an explanation for this. We are safe, Milo."

Milo was convinced that the lighthouse was haunted and I was starting to believe it, too. We tiptoed around, looking for intruders. Milo grabbed a broom on our way to the kitchen. "If we see the ghost, I will shoo it out the door and lock it behind her."

"I am not sure a locked door will keep a ghost out," I said as I pondered what we would do if we actually did find a ghost.

"How were you going to keep the mice from coming back in?" Milo asked.

"There is only one way to keep them from coming back. You have to take them really far away."

"Then I will shoo it all the way to the ocean and maybe it will fly away and find a new home," Milo said. He practiced waving the broom in the air, flinging it around like a sword.

Trembling, I peeked into the kitchen and finally discovered the culprit. Breathing a sigh of relief, I said, "The wind is blowing the door open and closed and that is why the rocking chair is rocking. Look, it is about to slam shut again."

BAM! Regardless of the warning, we still jumped about a mile into the air.

"I did not lock the door because I did not see a reason to. After all, we are the only ones living on the island."

"We are the only ones living on the island, as for non-living ghosts and monsters …" Milo said.

I inspected the door for any evidence of tampering but I didn't see anything strange or out of place. "It was absolutely the wind that caused all this fuss."

I peered outside. The nearby trees swayed in the breeze and the salty ocean air swirled my red hair all around. "It is a very windy day today. It must be the remnants of the storm from yesterday."

Milo crept up behind me and looked outside. "Maybe this time it was the wind. But I bet you anything that the girl in the painting is a ghost and she is determined to get us off her island!"

"Alright, I will take you up on that bet," I said with a mischievous smile. "If I win and we never find a ghost, then you owe me one dinner out at Pizza Neetza. I want a Greek salad with Italian dressing, large mac and cheese pizza, and two slices of key lime pie. I will pay, of course."

"Yum, tasty! And, if I win and we find a ghost?"

"If you win, I will owe you one dinner out at Pizza Neetza. We will order a Greek salad with ranch dressing, extra-large, extra cheese, cheese pizza, and a triple scoop chocolate sundae with chocolate sauce."

"You are making me hungry, Grammy!" Milo licked his lips and gazed out across the ocean toward home.

Dreaming about pizza, I closed the kitchen door

and locked it. "Since we don't have any pizza, how about some delicious dill pickles?" I used a spoon to pry open the pickle jar. "After our snack, let's head up to the top of the lighthouse."

Milo licked his lips and pulled out two spears. Salty brine dripped onto the floor as we munched on the crispy, crunchy pickles. Somehow we managed to polish off the entire jar in a matter of minutes.

"I never saw a way up to the lighthouse," Milo said as he wiped his hands on his shirt. He drank an entire glass of water and then promptly refilled it and drank that, too.

"The pickles are delicious but maybe a little salty," I said after taking a drink of water. "I think I saw a secret way up at the back of the house. Come on!"

At the back of the lighthouse there was a small, cozy, light-filled room with stairs leading to the upstairs bedrooms. "I don't see a door," Milo said.

"Are you sure you saw a way up?"

"Look at the wood panels over there," I said pointing to the far wall. "One of them is a different color than the others. And look at the anchor etched into the wood." I brushed my hand along the smooth wood, tracing the anchor and feeling the grooves from the beautiful carving.

"Look at this!" Milo exclaimed. Concealed on the wall next to a painting of a farm house covered in snow was a small handle with the same anchor etched into it.

"Pull it and see what happens," I said. I took a step back from the wall as Milo pulled down on the handle. Slowly, the wood panel rumbled open. We stepped inside and gazed up at a towering, windy staircase. The metal stairs spiraled upwards so high that we could not see the top. I was dizzy looking up even though my feet were firmly planted on the ground.

"The stairs have holes in them," Milo cried. His

face was white with fear, looking like he had just seen a ghost.

"I'm sure they are very sturdy. They were built that way. Just don't look down," I said as I gestured for him to begin his trek up to the top. "You go first. That way if you stumble, I will be there to catch you."

Milo took a deep breath, bringing some color back to his cheeks. He hugged the wall as he crawled slowly up the stairs on all fours. "There is no way I am doing this every day, Grammy!"

"Luckily we don't have to," I said. "With modern navigation, they don't need us to work the lights at the top." I half crawled, half walked behind Milo. I grasped the railing so tightly with my hands that they soon ached from the newly forming blisters.

"Oh, wow!" I cried, stepping onto the circular balcony at the top. It was the most spectacular, dazzling view I had ever seen. We could see for miles around in every direction. A pod of dolphins playfully leapt into the air, seemingly joyful that yesterday's storm had passed.

"What's that over there?" Milo asked. He pointed far out into the ocean where a black dot floated on top of the waves.

"Maybe some driftwood or possibly a boat?" I suggested, squinting to try and get a better look.

"Let's see if the telescope works," Milo said. A modern day telescope was bolted to the floor. Though it was battered from years of enduring the weather, it appeared to be in working order. It resembled the telescopes that line the top floor of Greenville's tallest building. Milo has used them many times so he skillfully focused the telescope on the object out at sea.

"Grammy, it's a boat! Weird!"

"Why is that weird?" I asked, squinting at the mouse-sized object. "There should be boats out there. It's an ocean."

"It is weird because it is a small row boat out on the open ocean. Oh no! I think it is going to capsize!"

"What? A row boat out in the ocean?" I took a turn peering through the telescope. Milo was right. I was shocked to discover children and adults on board the precariously looking boat.

"I think they are waving at us," I said. We waved back, hoping they could see us from so high up. "It looks like they are headed for the beach. The waves are pretty choppy today, but with their small boat, they may be able to make it onto shore."

"What are they doing out there?" Milo asked. He took one more look through the telescope.

"I have no idea. Let's go meet them on the beach and find out. It looks like they need our help!"

We warily made our way down the spiral staircase. I tried not to look down as we went, instead taking it one step at a time. My hands were slippery with sweat when I finally reached the last stair. "Thankfully our job does not require us to light the beacon at the top and watch for boats every day. I do not think I could it!"

"You would get used to it," Milo said optimistically. He gleefully skipped away. Milo's ability to adapt to any situation never ceases to amaze me.

I stretched my sore hands open and closed a few times, examining the marks left behind from my tight grip on the hand rail. I was about to turn around and look back at where we had come from, but stopped. "Always move forward, not back," I warned myself.

"Let's go meet the boat, Grammy!" Milo called, already far ahead of me.

"I'm coming!" I exclaimed.

Chapter 9

A row of razor sharp rocks jut out of the ocean and surround Ghost Island, forming a dangerous barrier. Only a few sea captains have ever attempted to land on the island. All have failed. They crashed into the rocks and were lost at sea.

Today, the small row boat had no choice but to maneuver its way through the dangerous rocks. We watched in horror as a piece of the boat tore off and floated away. It looked as if it may disintegrate at any moment, leaving the passengers out in the open ocean without any help nearby. We held our breath as the boat attempted the treacherous voyage to shore. It almost capsized twice but luckily it stayed upright against the crashing waves. The boat rocked back and forth uncontrollably and narrowly missed hitting a razor sharp rock head-on by only a few inches.

As soon as it broke through the rock barrier, I took off my shoes and raced out to meet it. I grabbed hold of the boat and helped pull it safely to shore. A man, woman, and five children wearily huddled together on the floor of the boat. The youngest was less than a year old, the oldest a teenager.

"Thank you so much," the man said, stepping out of the boat and holding it steady so the other passengers could safely disembark. His shirt was tattered and torn. Everyone looked hungry and tired.

"You're welcome," I said. "What are you doing out on the ocean in this rickety boat? Are you lost?"

"The country where we are coming from is in

turmoil and has become a dangerous place. The safest thing for me and my family was to leave and find a new home. This was the only boat we could find, and as you can see, we just barely fit. We brought along as much food and water as we could but it is running out. What a relief it was to see you at the top of the lighthouse!"

"I don't know what to say!" I exclaimed. "I ... I ..."

As I stumbled for the right words, Milo came to my rescue. "You can stay on the island with us. We have a ton of pickles, if you are hungry."

That made us all laugh and I regained my composure. "You are welcome on this island, of course. Please come up to the lighthouse so you can get something to eat and a good night's sleep. We have a little bit more to eat than just pickles!"

"Thank you! My name is Elsa," the woman said, reaching out to shake my hand.

"Hi Elsa. My name is Birdie and this is my

grandson, Milo. You probably won't want to live on this island because there isn't much here. We are the only people."

"And there might be a ghost or two!" Milo chimed in.

"Don't worry, there aren't any ghosts," I reassured our guests. "We aren't far from Greenville, which is where we live. We are on the island temporarily. I think you might be happier making your new home in Greenville."

"Greenville? What a friendly sounding town!" Elsa said.

Together we pulled the rowboat far onto the beach, ensuring it would not float away. Milo immediately became friends with a boy who was almost the same age and height as himself. They skipped up the path toward the lighthouse, acting as if they were long-lost friends.

"We can get some more food from the root cellar if you don't see anything here you like," I said as we crammed into the kitchen.

"Yum! Sourdough starter!" Elsa exclaimed, looking at a jar full of white, bubbly liquid that was sitting on the kitchen counter.

"Sourdough starter?" I asked, surprised. "Milo and I could not figure out what that was. Milo was convinced it was ghost food, so we just left it alone."

"It looks like it needs to be fed," Elsa said. She popped open the lid and immediately a strong, sour smell filled the room.

"Who tooted?" Milo asked, plugging his nose.

"Let's go outside and play," his new friend suggested after he finished giggling. "When my mom gets going with that sourdough stuff, it can get kind of stinky. We will come back when the food is ready. It might stink a little bit now, but soon it will taste delicious!"

I watched the boys disappear into the woods along a leaf carpeted trail. The sounds of screeching seagulls drowned out their footsteps as they hopped and skipped away. The smell of the sourdough starter brought my thoughts back to our work in the kitchen. "What do you mean it needs to be fed?" I asked.

"Sourdough starter is a living culture of bacteria and yeast. If you don't feed it more flour and water, it will die. This one still looks okay. I can tell because it is bubbling and it isn't black." Elsa stirred in equal amounts of flour and water. Then she got to work making sourdough flour tortillas.

She mixed flour, salt, baking powder, olive oil, sourdough starter, and water together until it formed a smooth dough. Then she covered it with a wet cloth.

"While it rests, let's prepare some vegetables to go with the tortillas," Elsa suggested.

"That sounds delicious!" I took her down to the root cellar. When we passed the painting of the girl, she appeared to be smiling politely. We filled a bucket with potatoes, carrots, onions, and pickled peppers before going upstairs.

Soon the kitchen was full of delicious smells that made my mouth water and my stomach grumble. After the vegetables were ready, we fried the tortillas in a cast iron skillet.

"I will call the boys in for dinner," I said. Walking outside, I found them examining an overturned rock.

"Look at how many different creatures are living under this rock, Grammy!" Milo exclaimed. He held a magnifying glass up to a millipede.

"Dinner is ready." Before I could say more the boys ran top-speed into the lighthouse.

Our night in the kitchen was filled with laughter, delicious food, and new friendships. It did not matter that we had just met and were from different parts of the world. The bonds we created would forever link us as friends and neighbors, no matter how far apart we lived.

After the most delicious dinner I had ever had, we cleaned up the dishes and I placed the food scraps in a bucket outside the front door. "I will take those to the compost tomorrow," I said, noticing how tired our new friends were.

"Before we go to bed, I should radio Captain Hook to see if he can escort you to Greenville tomorrow." I reached for the radio that was mounted on the wall next to the desk in the office.

"Captain Hook?!?!?" Elsa asked. Clearly she thought I was referring to THE Captain Hook.

"Not the one you are thinking of. His last name is Hook but he is not a pirate. He brought us safely to the island. He said if we needed anything, we should radio him for help."

"Oh, okay," Elsa said, looking relieved.

The captain answered my call almost instantly. I explained the situation and he was more than happy to help. "I will meet you at oh-five-hundred," the captain said, his voice crackling over the radio.

"Over and out."

"We better get to bed," I said. "We have an early morning tomorrow. The captain wants to get going early so that he has plenty of time to get you to Greenville during daylight hours."

Our new friends happily piled into the living room. Milo and I made our way upstairs to the bedrooms. After tucking Milo into his cozy bed, I collapsed in my own bed, exhausted from the busy day.

The morning came too quickly. Exhausted, I raced around the lighthouse, waking everyone up. Then I packed some snacks for the journey to Greenville. We made it to the beach only moments before the sound of a boat could be heard over the gentle, rolling waves.

At exactly oh-five-hundred, Captain Hook pulled Speed Racer as close to shore as he could get. After giving each other hugs, Elsa and her family stepped into their rowboat and maneuvered it out to where the captain waited patiently. Thankfully the water was smooth and clear and their boat effortlessly carried them without fear of capsizing. The captain greeted them with a smile and friendly wave before tying their boat to the back of his.

After their boat was secured, they climbed into Speed Racer and settled into their seats. As they prepared to leave, I shouted, "We hope to meet you in Greenville soon! Safe travels!" We watched until Speed Racer was out of sight.

"Why were you so nice to them? They were strangers to us but you treated them like family," Milo said.

"It is easy to forget that we live in a world full of different people and many of them need our help. Just because people may live far away or look different than us does not mean they are not our neighbors."

"Isn't a neighbor someone who lives next door

to you?" Milo asked, confused.

"That is one definition of a neighbor. But, the world is bigger than that and we are all living on this planet together."

"We are all in this together," Milo said. He jumped up onto a rock and turned to face the ocean.

"That's right. We are all in this together. And as neighbors, we should help each other. Everyone has unique and different gifts to offer. Everyone is important." I stepped up onto the rock and joined Milo. I gazed out at the vast, blue ocean contemplating how big our world seems but how small it actually is.

I picked up a piece of driftwood that was wedged between the rocks and examined its smooth surface. "Something powerful happens when we stop doing things for ourselves and start doing things for others."

"I definitely have a new friend for life!" Milo

said. "And now you know how to make tortillas! Come on, Grammy! Let's go treasure hunting!"

As Milo raced ahead of me, my thoughts turned to our new friends. I hoped that their journey would go smoothly and that the people of Greenville welcomed them with open arms. Though most of the people in Greenville are very friendly, I thought of one person in particular that may cause a few problems for them. Mr. Finch. Greedy Mr. Finch.

Chapter 10

In the morning, Beverly cheerfully left the city and drove to her post at the end of the Greenville River. This time she was prepared for an adventurous day. Trading her purse for a backpack, she filled it with guidebooks, a map, binoculars, trail mix, and water. She felt thrilled and exhilarated for the day ahead of her. It had been a long, long time since she felt such excitement.

She set up a chair near the edge of the river before commencing her explorations. Beverly was having so much fun that she was shocked when she looked at her watch and realized how much time had passed. It was nearing lunchtime so she decided to head back to her post near the river and take a break from her adventures.

Beverly ducked under a low-hanging tree branch, heavy with leaves and acorns. She stepped out of the woods and onto the dirt road. She was unpleasantly surprised to find Fable sitting in her chair with an umbrella in one hand and a frothy pink drink in the other.

"Why, Fable! This is a surprise!" Beverly said, doing her best to hide her disappointment.

"Have you solved the mystery yet?" Fable asked, impatiently. He took a long sip of his drink and swirled the straw around his glass, causing the ice cubes to clink together.

"Not yet," Beverly said. She sheepishly tucked a turkey feather into her backpack, not wanting Fable to see that the things she was carrying had absolutely nothing to do with the mystery of the Greenville River drying up.

"I was hoping you would be done by now because I need you back at the office." Fable dumped his nearly empty cup upside down. The ice cubes tumbled to the ground and a small puddle of pink liquid formed at Beverly's feet.

"At the office?" Beverly groaned. She could not hide the dread and dismay she felt. If Fable paid any attention to her, he would have noticed her doomed expression. Her smile was now long gone.

"Yes, playtime is over," Fable barked. "I expect you there within the hour. Go home and change first. You can't show up at my office looking like that."

"Like what?" Beverly said, now very annoyed. She looked down at her hiking shoes, khaki pants, and long sleeved button down shirt. She pulled the brim of her baseball cap further down onto her head.

"Like you are some kind of farmer or something. Anyway, hurry up! We have a problem."

"A problem?"

"Yes. Apparently, that crazy judge let a boat full of weird people come to Greenville. Not only did she let them come here but she helped them get here. I've been told that they are not good people. They look different than us and they might rob our stores and destroy our houses. We have to stop them."

"Are you talking about Judge Birdie?" Beverly asked.

"Yes, the crazy judge."

"She is not crazy. I am sure she had a good reason to let them come to Greenville."

"Are you taking her side?"

"I am not taking anyone's side. But I believe we should not assume they are here to do bad things."

"It does not matter what you think. I need you at the office. We need to board up the windows and blockade the doors. Then I need you to file a lawsuit so we can get those people thrown out of

Greenville."

Fable stood up from the chair and turned to leave. Beverly stomped her foot into the pool of pink liquid Fable had dumped on the ground. It splashed up and covered the back of Fable's dress pants, forming a pink polka dot pattern. Fortunately, he didn't notice.

"I expect to see you soon," Fable grumbled as he waddled to his car. Seeing the pink splatters covering the butt of his pants, Beverly could not help but giggle quietly. But as soon as his car was out of sight, she burst out in uncontrollable and hysterical laughter.

Beverly eventually stopped laughing and sat down. The thought of going back to work for Fable was unbearable. She munched on her trail mix, contemplating what she wanted her life to look like. There was only one thing she was sure of. She was not going to work for Fable Finch ever again.

She wasn't sure where life was going to take her,

but she was sure she was making the right choice. Beverly took her time finishing her trail mix before packing up her things. Even though Fable was never nice to her, she felt an obligation to at least inform him she was quitting her job. Effective immediately.

Chapter 11

Milo stood at the base of a walnut tree, staring at the lighthouse, looking mystified. He tossed a round, green walnut between his hands, occasionally stopping to smell the crisp, citrusy aroma.

"What are you looking at?" I asked.

"We made the ghost VERY angry!" Milo cried, pointing toward the lighthouse.

It was then that I saw the horrific mess that had stopped Milo in his tracks. My mouth dropped open and I let out a loud groan. "Oh, no! Look at this mess!"

Scraps of food were haphazardly flung across

the lawn, hanging from trees, and covering the stairs leading up to the lighthouse. We had not noticed it earlier that morning because it was still dark out. The now empty compost bucket was upside down about fifty yards from where I had left it the night before.

"This is all my fault. I should not have left the bucket on the steps overnight."

"I think we need to put the map back where we found it and forget about going on this treasure hunt," Milo whispered.

"A ghost did not make this mess," I said.

"Then what did? A goblin? A monster? A witch? A vampire?" Milo's eyes nearly popped out of his head as he tried to imagine the scariest possible scenario.

"How many different scary, pretend creatures do you think you can come up with?" I asked, amused by Milo's overactive imagination.

"I could probably go on forever. Why? Do you

need more options? How about a three-headed snake or a ..."

Before Milo could continue, I interrupted him. "You can be as creative as you want with your imagination but I do not think it will help you discover the culprit."

"You mean the creature we are living with is even scarier than anything I can imagine?" Milo asked, terrified.

"No, that's not what I mean. You seem to be on the wrong track here. I believe this mess was made by a raccoon. Or maybe a few raccoons. No ghosts, no monsters, and no three-headed snakes." Laughing, I bent down to examine a set of freshly made footprints in the mud.

"I do not think a little raccoon could make this big of a mess," Milo said. He was still confident that we were under a ghost attack and needed to run for our lives.

"Look closely at these footprints. The evidence

speaks for itself."

Milo tossed the walnut on the ground and suspiciously examined the set of freshly made tracks. "What if the ghost is just trying to trick us? Maybe she captured a raccoon and forced him to step in the mud to throw us off. Then, the ghost set up a trap inside the lighthouse and as soon as we step inside she is going to catch us and eat us!"

"Milo …" I began.

"Okay, fine. That probably didn't happen. But it would have been a lot cooler to tell my friends that we survived an attack by a giant, green-haired monster who had gleaming red eyes and ten heads."

"Let's clean up this mess so we can start our treasure hunt! Maybe we will find a monster with twenty heads and fifty eyes that magically appears when the treasure chest opens!"

With a glint in his eyes, Milo raced for a pile of potato peels. "The raccoons made a gigantic mess! It looks like they did this just for the fun of it!" He dumped the pile of potato peels into the compost bucket and raced for some uneaten, squished tomato peels that a raccoon had smeared all over a tree trunk. A half-eaten carrot hung from a tree branch. The sad remains of a trampled and partially munched upon tortilla were scattered across a lawn chair.

"Apparently they did not like their dinner choices." I collected the carrot from the tree and put it into the bucket. "It looks like the raccoons had a party out here last night!" I picked up an overturned chair and set it upright, examining the muddy footprints left behind on the armrest. "They are not very good at covering up their crime."

Milo laughed as he turned his attention to an overturned flower pot. The raccoon had dug up the flowers and the potting soil was spread across the ground. Milo did his best to put it all back together, though the purple flowers were wilted and partially broken.

"Naughty raccoons!" I said as I gave the sad looking flowers some water.

When we finished cleaning up the mess, I dumped the compost into the large cedar compost bin and joined Milo at the lighthouse.

"Why are you wearing ski goggles?" I asked, placing our now empty compost bucket on the ground next to the kitchen door.

"Because we might encounter a ghost who shoots lasers out of its eyes!" Milo said.

"I don't think ski goggles are going to protect you from laser shooting ghosts," I said, laughing. "Where did you find ski goggles?"

"I brought them from home," Milo said, clearly proud of himself and his thoughtful planning. "I also brought a wet suit. Maybe I should put that on, just in case we run into electromagnetic waves. Oh, and my knee pads might help if I have to try and escape a giant, hairy spider."

"No wonder your backpack was so heavy," I

said. "You can wear the goggles if you want but please leave the rest behind. All this monster busting gear is going to slow us down. It will take days to get to the treasure."

"We can't be slow when we face the monsters. So, I guess I will have to leave it behind." Milo grabbed a walking stick and a jar of pickles before fearlessly marching off down the path.

The map took us deep into a shadowy forest, moss carpeted the ground and the air smelled of decomposing leaves. The enormous, ancient tree branches blocked out the sunlight, intertwining from years of growth. Careful to duck under low branches and step over the dead, fallen trees, we cautiously made our way down a steep, muddy hill and into a dark ravine.

"According to the map we have to go in there," I said, pointing to a menacing gorge. The crooked trail at the bottom of the ravine was covered with boulders and fallen trees. The sides of the ravine were too steep to climb. Once we went in, we only had two choices. Keep going or turn back the way we came. There was no other way out.

Suddenly, a rock came loose and crashed down the steep, craggy hill. It landed with a bang at the bottom of the ravine, crushing everything in its path.

"This is going to be dangerous," I said. "Maybe we should turn back and look for a different route."

"You once told me that I should not let fear stop me in life," Milo said. Taking off his ski goggles, he inspected a cluster of orange fungi growing on a dead tree. "I think we should keep going. I think we can do this."

"Okay. But if things get too dangerous and I say we have to turn back, I don't want any arguing." I took his goggles and tucked them into his backpack next to the pickles.

"Fine, but just this one time," he said with a smile. Milo loved to argue, especially with me. If I said it was cold, he said it was hot. If I said it was late, he said it was early. If I said it was time to go inside, he said our outdoor adventures were just beginning. Although most of the time I loved this about him, today was not a day to question me.

Walking around boulders and ducking under trees, we cautiously made our way deeper and deeper into the darkness. Soon it felt like we were inside a mysterious, ghostly cave. It was dreadfully dark and nearly impossible to see where we were going. "Did you bring a flashlight?" I asked.

"Nope, but that would have been a good idea," Milo said. "I think I packed my light-up superhero watch. Maybe that will help?"

"We can try," I said, hopeful that even a little light would prevent us from stumbling and falling into the dark, murky abyss.

We stopped so Milo could search for his watch. All of a sudden, a great horned owl swooped down from a tree and flew only inches above our heads.

For a moment, all I could hear were the beautiful, rhythmic sounds of its flapping wings. A blur of brown and white feathers flew over us and gracefully landed upon the top of the tallest tree. Apparently satisfied that we were neither predators nor pray, it perched stoically on a branch, gazing at us with bright yellow eyes.

"That was so cool!" Milo exclaimed, beaming with admiration as he gazed back at the majestic bird.

"Watching the owl was treasure enough for me. If we do not find anything more, I will still call our adventure a success!"

"You know what, Grammy? For once I totally agree with you!" Milo found his watch buried deep within the pockets of his backpack. He held it up with triumph.

Pushing a button on the watch, the quiet forest was filled with a loud *VROOOM!* "Oops, wrong button!" Trying again, this time a flashing orange, green, and blue light appeared. It did not illuminate much but at least it might alert the forest creatures as to our presence.

"It's better than nothing," I said, giving Milo a reassuring grin.

The walls of the ravine inched closer and closer together as we lumbered along. Before long, we were forced to walk sideways and slide our bodies against the wet, rocky sides.

"If it gets any tighter in here, we are going to have to turn around." Because of my fear of small spaces, I was filled with terror and panic.

Out of nowhere, gushing water streamed out from cracks in the rocks and submerged the path with icy, cold water. As my panic escalated so did the terrifying thoughts running through my head. "What if we get stuck in here? What if a rock crashes down on us? What if I slip and fall and Milo can't help me? What if there is a five-headed monster who tries to eat us?" The further we went, the more irrational my thoughts became. Just as I was on the brink of losing control, a beam of light pierced the darkness, the path began to widen, and I was filled with hope.

"I think we are almost out, Grammy!" Milo exclaimed.

Though my water soaked shoes were heavy and awkward to move, the hope of getting out of the ravine renewed my strength and I swiftly put one foot in front of the other.

We came upon a tight bend in the path that prevented us from seeing what was to come. Milo skillfully maneuvered through the crevice and disappeared. My panic mounted as I tried to catch up with him. I squeezed through the crevice, fear forcing me to clamp my eyes firmly closed.

"Open your eyes, Grammy!" Milo's serene voice immediately put me at ease.

I pried my eyes open. I was enchanted by a graceful, sparkling waterfall gently splashing down a rocky overhang and bubbling its way down the path from which we had just come. A rainbow sprang up from the pool of turquoise water that formed at the bottom of the waterfall, leading me to believe we were, in fact, on the right path. The steep sides of the ravine gave way to rolling, grassy hills.

"We did it!" I exclaimed. Relief flooded over me and I realized I had been holding onto my backpack so tightly that the indentation of my fingers now formed a permanent decoration on the straps.

Milo dropped his backpack, took off his wet shoes, and jumped into the sparkling, shallow water. He stuck his head under the rushing waterfall, soaking his brown hair. Laughing, he cupped his hands into a bowl and collected the crisp water. With a glint in his eyes, he tossed the water at me. Instinctively, I turned and the water hit me in the back, soaking me through my shirt.

I kicked my shoes off and jumped in. Soon we were entangled in an epic water fight. Milo claimed he won, though I believe it was me. Exhausted, we plopped down on a soft mound of green grass and warmed ourselves in the sun.

"Let's eat!" Milo said. He got out a jar of pickles from his backpack, unscrewed the top, and pulled out a spear. He devoured it in two bites and then reached in for another.

"Did you bring anything other than pickles?" I asked, searching his backpack.

"Nope, just pickles and they are delicious!" He took another bite and a spray of pickle juice dripped all over his feet.

"Then for lunch today, we shall dine on pickles!" I plucked one from the jar and took a bite. A hungry squirrel smelled our delectable, salty snack and inched its way closer and closer, hoping we would share a bite or two.

Finally full, I wiped my hands on my shirt before pulling out the map. "We are almost there! We need to go in that direction for about a mile and then we should be at the beach." I pointed at a prairie full of wildflowers and buzzing bees. It looked much more inviting than the ravine and I was eager to move forward.

"Onward!" Milo yelled, pointing a stick in the direction we needed to go. Recharged from our pickle break, we raced out of the gorge and up a rolling hill, coming upon bright blue sky and a salty, gentle breeze.

Chapter 12

As Beverly drove into town, she contemplated how to tell Fable that she was quitting her job. She believed that honesty was always the best policy. Unfortunately, Fable could be a little snippy sometimes. To be fair, he was snippy most of the time but Beverly believed that deep down Fable had a good heart. He just had not discovered it yet.

She found an empty parking stall on Main Street, locked her car doors, and walked one block to the office. She was surprised to discover a charming new restaurant opening next to Fable's office. "That looks like it is going to be good!"

As she admired the freshly painted building and

outdoor tables, Fable hastily emerged from his office and lumbered outside. He was dragging a pile of wooden boards with one hand and holding a hammer and nails with his other.

"Fable, what are you doing?" Beverly asked, confused.

Fable dropped the boards and they tumbled to the ground, landing in a haphazard, chaotic heap. It reminded Beverly of what it felt like to work for Fable. Crazy, turbulent, frenzied, and hectic.

"I thought I told you to change your clothes before coming to work!" he commanded. He rolled his eyes with disapproval before intently inspecting the hammer. "How does this thing work?"

"That's a hammer, Fable," Beverly said, astonished. She knew he was not the most skilled of attorneys but she was surprised to discover how little he knew about simple life skills.

"I know it's a screwdriver! I could not find any instructions at the hardware store on how to use this thing."

"It's a hammer not a screwdriver."

"That is what I said," Fable snapped. Clearly he had absolutely no idea what he was doing. "Since you seem to be the expert, you will board up the windows. Do not leave a single one unprotected."

"Why are you boarding up the windows? Is there a hurricane coming?" Beverly asked. A curious crowd of spectators formed around the commotion, wondering if they needed to check the weather.

"Yes, in fact there is a hurricane coming … a hurricane of people who are storming into our peaceful town. And they are going to steal from us, take all of our jobs, and commit crimes. Who knows what else these criminals are going to do. We have to protect ourselves. I want my law office boarded up so that nobody can break in!"

"Why would anyone want to break into your office? What are they going to steal? Old cheese puffs and half eaten doughnuts?" Beverly laughed.

Just then, a woman emerged from the newly painted restaurant next door. Smiling she approached the small crowd. "Hello! My name is Elsa. My family and I recently moved to Greenville. We are incredibly thankful for the opportunity to make this our new home. Everyone has been very welcoming and my children are enjoying their new friends."

Elsa paused and waved to her children who were happily playing at the park across the street. "Opening day for our restaurant is tomorrow! We are having a buy one get one free special all day. We specialize in sourdough breads, pizzas, and tortillas."

The crowd murmured with excitement. "Sourdough pizza? That sounds delicious," Beverly said. "Welcome to Greenville. Most of the people here are quite friendly." She gave Fable a warning look, hoping he would keep his mouth closed. Tightly closed.

Fable scowled, turned his back to the crowd, and began pounding a board over a window. There was only one problem. He forgot to use a nail. When he stepped back to admire his handiwork, the board crashed to the ground.

The crowd soon dispersed and Elsa went back to work. Beverly cleared her throat and commenced what she believed was going to be a difficult, but necessary, discussion. "Fable, I need to talk to you."

"We do not have time to chitchat today. You heard what that woman said. She is planning to take over our town. We have to save ourselves! We have to save Greenville!" He scrutinized the hammer, confused as to why the board had fallen to the ground.

"That is not what she said and I refuse to be part of your lies any longer."

Fable's face turned an angry, bright red and his eyes narrowed into thin slits. "Lies?"

"Maybe you do not mean to lie but you

frequently distort the truth. Elsa seemed very nice. She said nothing about taking over Greenville or hurting anyone. I am looking forward to trying the food at her restaurant and I plan to be there on opening day!"

"You can go in but you might not come back out!" Fable boomed. He frantically returned to his work. This time using a nail, he pounded his hammer with such force that the board split and tumbled to the ground in pieces.

"This is exactly why I will not work for you anymore," Beverly said with authority.

"Excuse me?" Fable slowly turned away from his work, looking worried and bringing his eyebrows together in a way that Beverly had never seen before.

Looking Fable squarely in the eyes, Beverly boldly and confidently continued. "I quit. Effective immediately."

"You can't quit! I need you!" Fable boomed.

The worry on his face was now replaced with the look of anger and rage that Beverly knew so well.

"Then you should of thought about that sooner. You have been treating me poorly since the day I started and I have had enough. I deserve to be treated with respect."

Fable looked dumbfounded, clearly unaware of his own behavior. Not feeling an ounce of sympathy, Beverly continued. "I wish nothing but the best for you. I hope you learn from this experience and treat your next assistant better … that is if you can find another assistant."

"But … wait … no! This can't be happening!" Fable stammered. "How about a raise? I can offer you an extra ten dollars a year. That's pretty good! Trust me, you won't get an offer like that from anyone else."

"I wouldn't stay even if you offered me an extra million dollars a year! Sorry Fable, but in my heart I have already moved on." With that, Beverly turned and walked back to her car. She felt like she was walking on air and noticed a new bounce in her step.

As soon as she got home, Beverly searched online for homes for sale in the country. To her delight, she found a honey bee farm on the market and it was only an hour outside of Greenville. The honey bee farmers wanted to retire and wished to sell to somebody who would love and care for their bees as they had.

The quaint farmhouse stood on thirty acres of prairie and forest land. A bubbling brook ran through part of the property. "Perfect!" Beverly exclaimed as she dialed the farmer's phone number.

Indeed it did turn out to be perfect. Before long, Beverly found herself happily unpacking her things and settling into her new life as a beekeeper. There was much to learn but she was confident she could do it. The honey bees were now her "boss" and she loved going to work every day.

Meanwhile, though it took some time, Fable finally figured out how to use a hammer and nails. Eventually he finished boarding up his office. Stepping back to admire his handiwork, he realized he had boarded up the door and now there wasn't a way to get inside. "This is all Beverly's fault. If she was a good assistant, she would have put the boards up for me and she would have remembered to leave a way in. She is so selfish, leaving me to do the dirty work!"

Fable pulled and pulled but the boards were nailed so tightly to the door that they did not budge. Exhausted and frustrated, he sat down in front of his office and fought back tears. A kind pedestrian took pity on him and showed him how to use the back of the hammer to remove the nails.

Fable went back to work tearing down the boards that covered his office door. It was dark by the time he finished so he decided that the best thing to do would be to go home and go to bed. In his haste, he left his office door unlocked and wide open. If anyone had any desire, they could have walked right in and helped themselves to his beloved cheese puffs.

Chapter 13

Milo and I gathered our courage and climbed one last steep, rocky embankment. With relief, we emerged onto a white sandy beach. The deep royal blue ocean twinkled under the sun. The gentle waves rhythmically swept over the sand and left new designs in their wake.

"According to the map, the treasure should be right about here," Milo said, pointing to a spot on the sand. "But, all I see is sand and shells."

"Maybe this beach is the treasure. It is so beautiful and peaceful here." A wave of calm washed over me. Nothing else seemed to matter. My everyday problems back in Greenville seemed so meaningless and inconsequential as I watched the rise and fall of the waves.

"Usually when people go treasure hunting, they have to dig for it," Milo said. He put his backpack on the sand and pulled out a small, orange shovel. He marked a circle in the sand around where he expected the treasure to be. Then he started to frantically dig.

"Slow down, Milo! We aren't in a rush," I said, trying to avoid being hit by flying sand.

The deeper we went, the harder it was to dig. The sand became heavier and heavier until it eventually turned into thick, dark, mud. "I don't know if there is anything in here," I said. I was covered in sand and my hands ached from the digging.

"We can't stop! At least not yet," Milo said, determined to continue on.

"Okay, we don't need to quit yet," I said, not wanting to disappoint him. "But you should be prepared for the possibility that there isn't a treasure. I still think that maybe this immaculate beach is the treasure. Just look at how beautiful it is. I wish we could stay here forever!"

Milo's unexpected scream startled me out of my daydream. "GRAMMY!!! I think I found something!"

Milo threw his shovel behind him and dropped to his knees. Digging furiously, he covered us with thick, wet mud. Eventually he pulled out a box, stood up, and rubbed off as much mud as he could.

"We found it!" I said, astonished. I rushed over to Milo and we plopped down in the warm sand, sitting so close that our knees touched. His trembling hands grasped the box and his eyes sparkled with excitement. Looking into his big, brown eyes, I said, "You can do the honors."

"What if I unleash a terrifying monster who gobbles us up?"

"I think the box is too small to hold a monster,"

I said.

"Then maybe there is a mini monster that lives inside who carries a giant monster curse and will turn us into ..."

Before his imagination could go any further, I popped open the lid. Thankfully, a monster did not fly out. Nor were we exposed to a giant monster curse.

"What in the world is all of this?" Milo asked as he shuffled through the treasure chest.

"I ... I ...don't ... know," I stammered, bewildered.

The box was filled with neatly folded cream colored pieces of paper. Hidden at the bottom of the box was a thick, yellow envelope, seemingly stuffed full with more treasure. I picked up the paper from the top of the pile and read it out loud.

What you sow is what you grow.

"Is that a clue?" Milo asked. "I hope that is not the treasure!"

One by one I opened the pieces of paper. They all contained different sayings.

In a world where you can be anything, be kind.

A generous heart and a life of giving makes the world a better place.

Do not just speak kind words. Live by them.

This too shall pass. Nothing is permanent.

Happiness comes when you appreciate what you already have.

Kindness never decreases by being shared.

Be you. Everyone else is taken.

"The treasure chest is full of wisdom!" I said, enchanted and overjoyed by the beautiful words contained within the silver box.

"Wisdom? That's boring," Milo said, shrugging his shoulders and looking like he was already prepared to move on to something else in life.

"There is nothing more valuable than learning how to live a good life. Gold, riches, jewels, and money are meaningless compared to this," I said.

"There are many people in life who have a lot but their hearts are cold and they are not happy.

Money does not bring happiness. Money does not bring wisdom. Money often brings ruin and heartache. It is better to live a life full of love and kindness than it is to fill your life with material riches."

"I guess so," Milo grumbled, still unwilling to accept my philosophy on life's treasures.

"What would have happened if this box was full of gold?"

"We would be rich!" Milo cried. "I would buy myself a new train set, and a new race car, and a new basketball hoop, and a new ..."

Holding up my hand, I pulled Milo from his thoughts. "But you already have so many things. Why do you need more things? Besides, you would quickly become bored with your new things and want to buy more new things. Eventually you would run out of money and feel worse than before you had it all."

"Maybe," Milo said, beginning to accept that

money would not buy him happiness.

"Grammy! We forgot to check what was inside the envelope." Renewed with hope for treasure, Milo brightened and dug in the chest, pulling out the old, crumbled envelope. "I hope it's not full of more wisdom."

"I hope it is full of more wisdom. We need to study these words and inscribe them into our hearts so we become the best people we can be." I opened the envelope and discovered a mound of smaller envelopes.

With his eyes closed, Milo squealed, "Did you find gold, Grammy? Please tell me you found gold!"

"No, I did not. I found something better than gold! Open your eyes, Milo."

"Gross, Grammy! Are you holding mouse poop?" Milo asked. He scrunched up his nose and backed away from me.

"No," I giggled. "These are seeds! Heirloom seeds for a type of cilantro that is more than one hundred years old!" I carefully put the small, round seeds back in the envelope before looking through the others. "Look at all of the tomato varieties! And squash! And here are some basil, pumpkin, sunflower, beet, and cucumber seeds. We are rich, Milo! Rich!"

"Really? Are they worth a lot of money?"

"Didn't you hear anything I said about money, Milo? No, we are not rich with money. We are rich with something better than that. We get to take these seeds home and plant a beautiful heirloom garden. And at the end of the season, we will have the privilege of enjoying our bountiful and delicious harvest!"

"You don't know how to garden."

"I will learn. No. We will learn. We will plant the seeds together and watch them grow. We will be rich with experiences and delicious food by next fall!"

"That sounds fun!" Milo said, forgetting about

his disappointment. "I want to do the watering. I love to play with the hose. You can do the weeding and I will try not to get you wet when I water." His eyes twinkled as he imagined "accidently" spraying me with the garden hose.

The sun was low in the sky and for the first time that day I thought about the passing of time. "We need to start heading back home. It will be dark soon," I said. I packed up our treasure and started filling in the hole in the sand.

Milo grabbed his shovel and helped. When we were done, the beach looked almost as pristine as how we had found it. The only remaining evidence of our intrusion were our footprints but the wind and waves were quickly erasing them.

"I don't want to go back through the ravine, Grammy." Milo said. He pushed the shovel into his backpack and zipped it closed.

"I don't either. Maybe we can find another way back? After all, the island isn't that big. How hard could it be to find the lighthouse?"

I turned around in circles a few times, contemplating which way to go. Unsure of how to decide, I closed my eyes, spun around three times, and pointed my finger. "We will go that way!" I declared, hopeful that my technique would get us safely back to the lighthouse before dark. It turned out that finding another way back was not a good idea. In fact, it was much worse than I ever could have imagined.

Chapter 14

"Well Milo, this may not have been the best idea," I said, rolling my eyes at my own foolishness. Though we had been walking for three hours, we were not any closer to the lighthouse than when we started. Somehow, we managed to walk in a complete circle and were back on the beach where we had dug for treasure. The same beautiful beach that only hours earlier had given me such joy was now making angry. Very angry.

"Nice job, Grammy. I knew you were not very good with directions but I didn't know you were this bad!" Milo keeled over and laughed so hard that tears streamed down his cheeks.

"Laugh all you want Milo but this was partly your idea, too!"

"Yeah, but you are in charge," Milo managed to say between giggles.

"We need to get moving, and fast. It will be dark soon."

Milo immediately stopped laughing. "Maybe we should retrace our steps through the ravine?"

Watching the golden sun sink below the pink horizon filled me with panic and dread. It was about to get dark. Very, very dark.

"It is too dangerous to go through the ravine in the dark. We barely made it during the day. We have to find another way. If worse comes to worst, we can sleep under a tree tonight."

"Under a tree?" Milo said, scrunching up his face.

"Or under a bush. Or how about on top of a log? Maybe a soft, comfy patch of grass would be nice? You can take your pick between all of nature's delightful beds!" I said, trying to sound enthusiastic about our sleeping accommodations for the night.

"Let's just get going. With any luck, we will find the lighthouse," Milo grumbled.

"Let's try this direction," I suggested, pointing in the opposite way from which we had come.

Milo parted the tall prairie grass and took a step into the towering plants. I followed closely behind. The plants brushed against my arms and legs, tickling me as I went. The thunder of lapping waves grew quieter and quieter as we moved away from the beach. Finally, we reached the edge of the prairie and came upon a stream. Exhausted, we sat down on an enormous, flat rock.

"How about we sleep here for the night?" I suggested. "This rock sure is cozy!" I stretched out across the rock and stared up at the emerging stars. Thankfully the moon was full and bright and the night was not nearly as dark as it could have been.

Though I was ready to close my eyes and go to

sleep, off in the distance I heard Milo exclaim, "Grammy, you need to come take a look at this!"

"Can't it wait until tomorrow?" I asked. Entranced by the night sky, I continued to lie on my back, examining the vastness of the universe before me.

"No, it can't! Get up and get over here!"

Detecting the urgency in his voice, I dragged myself up and grudgingly went to see what was so important. Even though it was dark, it immediately became clear that we had a problem. A big, terrifying problem.

"Human footprints!" I exclaimed. Though I knew we were sharing the island with many different creatures, it never occurred to me that we might be sharing it with other humans.

"They aren't mine," Milo said.

"They aren't mine," I added.

Curiosity was the only thing that prevented me from grabbing Milo's hand and running away as fast as possible. I needed to find out who else was on the island.

"We need to get out of here!" Milo whispered. His eyes darted back and forth as he searched for a band of attack pirates.

I held a finger to my lips, indicating for Milo to be quiet while I surveyed the surrounding forest. Terrified, I expected to find pirates ready to attack. Or worse, horrible red monster eyes staring at me. But of course, I did not see anything.

"Perhaps someone came over on a boat for the day. Or maybe these are our footprints from our first circle around the island. Or maybe a raccoon stole our shoes and these are, after all, raccoon footprints!" My last idea made us laugh and we temporarily felt better.

"Maybe pirates are here and they are looking for treasure! Maybe the ghost is following us and made the footprints to scare us! I'm out of here!" Milo turned and tried to bolt but I grabbed his arm just in time.

"I think we should follow the footprints and see where they lead," I said bravely.

"I am not doing that," Milo said. He stubbornly planted his feet firmly on the ground and grabbed tightly onto a tree branch, making it clear that I was not going to win this battle easily.

"If we turn around, there is no chance of getting to the lighthouse tonight. We will be stuck out here all night … in the dark … possibly with a group of attack pirates after us and our treasure!"

Milo took a few minutes to consider his options before making a decision. "Fine. Have it your way. But, I hope for once in your life you are right about something!"

"I hope so, too."

Our eerie walk in the dark through an unfamiliar forest would never escape my memory. For years to come, I knew I would think back to this moment in our lives, remembering our bravery. The dark night sky was thick with fog but the silver moon lessened the inky blackness. The music of crickets filled the night with rhythmic chirping. Occasionally an owl called in the distance, reminding us that we were definitely not alone.

"Milo, look," I whispered. A pile of rocks was skillfully and artfully arranged into a tower that resembled a pirate ship.

"Whoa," Milo whispered back. He picked up a small, round stone that had toppled to the ground and placed it back onto the formation. Stepping back, it was clear that the stone was meant to be the cannon of the ship.

"Obviously pirates made this! We are doomed!" Milo exclaimed, goosebumps covering his arms.

Suddenly, an unfamiliar voice resonated from behind. "I made that yesterday." The raspy, crackly voice pierced through me like a dagger and I froze, paralyzed with fear.

"AAAAHHHHHHH!" Milo screamed, causing

me to jump.

"AAAAAAAHHHHHHHHHH!!" I screamed even louder.

"AAAAAAHHHHHHHHH!" the unfamiliar voice bellowed.

Our voices joined together, sounding a lot like a choir of unskilled musicians. The obnoxious sound echoed off the hills and silenced the night creatures. I would not be surprised if they packed up and left in search of a quieter home.

Anticipating the worst possible scenario, I pushed Milo behind me and spun around to face my certain demise. Only a few feet away, standing upon a moonlit rock, was a woman. Her pearly-white dress fluttered in the wind. Her wispy, long gray hair was tied up into a messy bun piled on top of her head. She looked oddly familiar, though I could not figure out why.

"Who are you and what are you doing on this island?" I demanded with authority. After all, I was in charge of Ghost Island. I could call the captain and tell him to bring the police. That is, if I could find the lighthouse and the CB radio.

"Are you a..a..a..ghost? Or, a pirate?" Milo stammered, peeking out from behind me.

"No I am not a ghost or a pirate. My name is Lady Gray and I am the lighthouse keeper. I believe I am the one who should be asking, what are *you* doing here?"

"You are Lady Gray?" I asked, astonished.

"The ghost of Lady Gray!" Milo squealed. "Run, Grammy! Run!"

"You don't need to run! I am not a ghost!"

We didn't run away, but we also didn't relax. I looked at Milo, Milo looked at me, and neither of us had any idea what to do next.

"What are you two doing here?" Lady Gray's quiet, raspy voice was now louder and angrier because of our repeated accusations.

"Sorry, we didn't mean to offend you. We are

shocked to find you alive and well. The Park Patrol reported you missing and they needed someone to take over your job until they could find you. My grandson and I volunteered to be wickies for one month," I said.

Lady Gray's sincere smile put me at ease and I felt my fear dissolving like melting snow under the warmth of the sun. "Disappeared? I didn't disappear. I have been here all along. I must have lost track of time and missed the Park Patrol's monthly visit to the island. I did not mean to cause so much trouble!"

"What are you doing out here in the woods? Why haven't we seen you at the lighthouse?" I asked.

"The mice were driving me crazy. Their pink twitchy tails, black beady eyes, and scrawny feet finally lost their charm. So, I made a deal with them. I told them to live in the lighthouse while I lived out here!"

"The mice kicked you out of the lighthouse?" Milo asked, horrified. "Are they pirate mice? Maybe, monster mice?"

"No, they are just ordinary, brown mice," Lady Gray laughed. "I am used to sharing the lighthouse with a few mice. However, this year there were so many that they were taking over the place. Every single inch of it. One morning, I woke up and found a mouse curled up on my pillow, sound asleep and snoring. That was the last straw! I packed up a few of my things and moved out. I have been happily living out here and they have been happily living in the lighthouse. I have not seen a single mouse since relinquishing my accommodations to them. I am delighted to report that my deal with the mice was a success and they are completely leaving me alone!"

"Is that why you wrote that strange note in your journal?" Milo asked.

"Oh, you saw my note? Sorry about that," Lady

Gray said, laughing. "I could not take one more day with those creatures. Are they sleeping in the bed? Is there a drop of food left in the place? Is there mouse poop everywhere?"

"We had a few problems," I said, shivering from my memories of the sneaky mice scrambling about the kitchen.

"If Grammy woke up and found a mouse curled up next to her, she would have jumped in the ocean and swam back to Greenville," Milo said, giggling.

Lady Gray showed us her campsite. A cozy, one-person tent was nestled under a towering pine tree. A cast iron tripod cooking pot stood over a crackling fire. A delicious smelling vegetable stew bubbled inside the pot and a recently used neon green beach towel was draped over a tree branch. I could see why Lady Gray preferred her outdoor accommodations over the mouse infested lighthouse.

Lady Gray uncovered a bowl of freshly picked

red raspberries and gave it to Milo. He quickly devoured the juicy, ripe berries. Picking up on our hunger, she filled two blue bowls with the vegetable stew. We gratefully enjoyed the savory, autumn-colored stew while gazing up at the stars. Under normal circumstances Milo would have complained about eating kale and broccoli but tonight he gobbled it up.

"Lady Gray, would you mind having two guests for the evening? Milo and I would be so grateful if you allowed us to curl up by your toasty, warm fire. That is preferable to the rock we were considering earlier, right Milo?"

Before he could answer, Lady Gray said, "Why would you sleep on a rock?"

"Because we are totally and completely lost!" I told Lady Gray about the treasure map in the root cellar, our adventures to find the treasure, and our complete and utter failure at finding our way back to the lighthouse.

Lady Gray laughed. "How on earth did you get lost on the island? It is so small!"

"Grammy is not very good with direction!" Milo said.

"Did you find the treasure?" Lady Gray asked, excitedly. The silver moonlight reflected off her twinkling blue eyes as she waited impatiently to hear our story.

"We did! We were delighted to find that the treasure chest contained a very unusual and valuable treasure."

"So my treasure was a success?" Lady Gray asked.

"You hid the treasure?" Milo asked.

"Yes, I did!" We looked confused so Lady Gray explained herself. "As you know, the mice were driving me crazy. I started thinking that it might be time to pass my job along to somebody else. Preferably, somebody who really loves mice. I thought it would be so much fun to leave behind all that I learned over my many years of island life."

"That explains the initials L.G. on the map!" I exclaimed.

Lady Gray laughed as she settled in next to the crackling fire. Then she continued with her story. "One sunny morning, I was tending to my beloved garden when it dawned on me that a perfect and priceless treasure lay right in front of my eyes. The fruit and vegetable varieties I was growing have been on the island for at least one hundred years and are found nowhere else in the world!"

Lady Gray paused to watch a shooting star zoom across the dark night sky. After the fiery, blue streak disappeared, she continued. "This got me thinking, and before I knew what I was doing, I had set up the entire treasure hunt. I am so happy you enjoyed it!"

"Oh, brother," Milo said. "I was hoping pirates hid the treasure."

"Sorry to disappoint you, but it was me."

"We still can't rule out that the island is haunted," Milo said. He really wanted to tell his friends that he survived unimaginable perils during his time on the island.

"Why do you think the island is haunted?" Lady Gray asked.

"There is a painting of a girl in the stairwell leading down to the root cellar and I am sure she is a ghost haunting the island," Milo said.

Lady Gray laughed. "I already told you I am not a ghost!"

Confused, I asked, "Are you the girl in the painting?"

"Yep, that's me! My mother was an artist and she painted it many years ago. As you may have noticed, I have loved pirate ships since I was a child."

"So the lighthouse isn't haunted?" Milo asked, disappointed.

"Not that I know of," Lady Gray said.

"Well, then it still could be. Maybe there is an orange monster that lives in the lighthouse and only comes out at night!"

I let Milo continue his monster daydreams while I spoke with Lady Gray. "How do we get back to the lighthouse?"

"We are very close to it." She pointed to a tree covered hill. The old-growth trees were so tall and vast that they completely covered the horizon, preventing us from seeing through. "It is right over that hill."

"Really," I said, astonished.

It was abundantly clear that I still had no idea where I was so Lady Gray offered to help. "I will walk back with you."

"Thanks!" I said with relief. Lady Gray poured water on the fire. It sizzled and smoked as the flames went out. Then we set off for the lighthouse. I was expecting a long, difficult hike but it only took five minutes to get there.

"We were this close all along yet never able to find our way," Milo remarked. He shook his head at me and we laughed, partly out of relief to be home and partly about our foolishness.

"Good thing we ran into you," I said to Lady Gray. "Who knows how long we would have been wandering around the island."

"Knowing us, probably for the rest of our lives. We would have turned into the ghosts that haunt the island." Milo floated around the yard, weaving in and out of the trees, pretending to be a ghost.

Lady Gray left without coming inside. She said she was not ready to face the mice quite yet. She returned early the next morning, just as the sun was peeking over the horizon. She promptly radioed the captain and they laughed about the misunderstanding. He said he would let the Park Patrol know she was alive and well.

Because Milo and I were no longer needed as wickies, Captain Hook agreed to pick us up the following morning for our return journey to Greenville. Of course, he wanted us ready at oh-five-hundred.

Lady Gray showed us her exquisite garden. An apple tree was the crown jewel and stoically grew in the center, heavy with crisp, red fruit. She gave us invaluable advice on how to start an heirloom garden which left me confident we would succeed in our gardening ventures.

Milo showed Lady Gray his still empty mouse trap contraption. Though it had not caught a mouse, Milo was positive it would help keep the mice population in check.

"May we go up to the top of the lighthouse one more time," Milo asked after lunch.

"Absolutely!" Lady Gray and I said in unison.

Lady Gray went first and climbed the winding stairs with ease, exceptionally skilled from her years of work on the island. On the other hand, Milo and I slowly half-crawled, half-walked up the stairs, trembling with fright.

"This view never gets old," Lady Gray said as she stood admiring the vast, wondrous ocean.

"It is absolutely spectacular," I said.

Milo intently observed the world around him through the telescope, not saying a word. Several minutes of silence passed before Milo cried out with alarm. "I think I just solved the mystery, Grammy!"

"Honey, remember? I was with you when we found Lady Gray."

"Not that mystery! The one about the Greenville River! I think I know why it is running dry!"

Chapter 15

Fable was grumpy and cross when he woke up
the next morning. "Maybe Beverly is over her
temper tantrum and will be back at work today," he
grumbled as he clumsily attempted to make a pot of
coffee. His first attempt failed because he forgot to
add the coffee grounds which resulted in a pot of
hot water. His second attempt wasn't much better.
He overloaded the pot with too many coffee
grounds so the water barely got through. He was
forced to wait while a very slow trickle of thick,

black coffee pooled in the carafe.

Two hours later, Fable finally made it in to the office. His jaw dropped open when he discovered that his office door was unlocked and wide open.

"Somebody broke into my office!" he bellowed. "I bet it was the intruders who are trying to take over Greenville."

Without even checking to see if anything was missing, he stormed over to the recently opened restaurant, prepared to accuse the owners of theft. However, the moment he opened the restaurant door, the most delicious smell overpowered him and he abruptly froze so as to savor the delightful aroma.

The restaurant was packed full of customers. There wasn't an empty table in the entire restaurant. Near the front, Beverly happily sipped a cup of coffee while reading the newspaper. As Fable watched with his mouth watering, a waiter delivered a plate piled high with pancakes topped with fresh berries and whipped cream.

"Good morning!" Elsa cheerfully greeted Fable. "Unfortunately, all of our tables are full but it shouldn't be too long before one opens up."

"Actually … um … I was wondering if you broke into my office last night?" His words did not sound nearly as cross as he wished them to. His rage was replaced with hunger and he wished desperately for a stack of pancakes.

"Of course not!" Elsa said, frowning. "I would never do something like that!"

Overhearing the commotion, Beverly quickly came to Fable's aid. "I have to apologize for my boss … I mean, my old boss. He sometimes says things he should not but underneath it all, he isn't a bad guy. Right Fable?" Beverly nudged Fable with her elbow.

"Yeah, yeah," he grumbled. "I'm working on it." Evidently, Elsa forgave Fable and handed him a menu.

"Why don't you join me?" Beverly suggested. She gestured toward her table. Before Fable could protest, Beverly ushered him to an empty chair.

For the first time ever, Beverly and Fable actually enjoyed spending time together. They spent the morning chatting about the weather and the delicious food.

Shockingly, Fable paid for Beverly's breakfast. "I think I owe you for all the stuff I have put you through," Fable said quietly, looking down at his polished black shoes.

Beverly drank the last sip of her freshly squeezed orange juice. "Thank you, Fable. What brought about this nice change?"

"I did not realize how great of an assistant you were until you were gone. In fact, I kind of thought of you as a friend." Fable left a generous tip at the table before placing his napkin on his plate and standing up from his chair.

"Wow! I'm speechless!" Beverly exclaimed. She

accompanied Fable on the short walk to his office.

"Why do you think somebody broke in?" Beverly asked with alarm. She examined the office door for signs of a break-in but didn't see any.

"Because the door was open and unlocked," Fable said. He turned the unlocked door handle, flung the door open, and stuck his head inside. "Is anyone in here?" His voice rumbled off the office walls but no other sound was heard.

"Fable, did you close and lock it last night when you left?"

"No. Why would I do that? That is your job."

"I don't work for you anymore, remember?" Beverly said, patting him on the shoulder.

"Oh yeah, I forgot. I bet I left my door unlocked every night this week! And the week before that, and the week before that ..."

Fable looked so sad and lost that Beverly actually felt sorry for him. "Fable, I could use a little help on my honey bee farm and I think you might be the perfect person for the job. Every day I have to inspect my hives. And extracting and bottling the honey is a lot of work for one person. Plus, I have a stand at the farmer's market where I sell my honey every Saturday. Come to think of it, I really could use a full time employee."

"Me? Work for you?" Fable asked, confused.

Beverly couldn't decide if Fable was annoyed or pleased with her proposal. "Yes. You work for me." She took a step back, ready to run if Fable got mad. "But I have one condition. You have to come to work in a good mood. If you don't, I will instruct my bees to sting you."

Fable was silent for several minutes, deep in thought about the opportunity for a career change. "You know, I have been thinking about taking a break from practicing law and well … I admit I do miss your company. Plus, I don't have any clients right now or even any foreseeable prospective clients. So, I suppose my answer is … yes!" Fable was so surprised by his decision that he had to sit down and take several long, deep breaths.

Delighted, Beverly gave Fable a hug. "I will see you tomorrow morning! Oh, and Fable? Don't forget to close and lock the office door tonight when you leave!" Beverly walked to her car feeling proud that she forgave Fable and was giving him another chance.

Over time, Beverly and Fable slowly became expert beekeepers while happily working side-by-side. Though they still had a few squabbles, for the most part, they enjoyed working together. As time went by, Fable began to appreciate the natural world around him. Gradually, the old, greedy Fable was replaced with a person he barely recognized as himself. Though it was not an easy road, he was pleased with the changes he made. He was devoted to making the world a better place. One child, one leopard, one bee, one flower at a time.

Chapter 16

"Grammy, a factory is diverting the water from the Greenville River!" Milo exclaimed. He stepped away from the telescope so I could take a look.

Not far from the edge of the Greenville River was a large, brown factory that clung precariously to a hillside. A line of tall smoke stacks spewed thick, black smoke high into the air. A black wrought iron fence topped with barbed wire surrounded the factory. From the ground, the factory would be hidden from view but was visible to us because we were up so high. Someone had redirected the river so that it forked off and formed a pool directly in front of the factory. The redirected water disappeared into a concealed, secret tunnel.

"I think you might be right, Milo. As soon as we get home, we are going to figure out what is going on!"

It took some time, but eventually we grew tired of searching the horizon for evidence and agreed it was time to say goodbye to the spectacular view and crawl our way down the stairs. Though the descent was terrifying, a wave of sadness spread over me the moment I reached the bottom stair, knowing I may never see the view from the top of the lighthouse ever again.

The rest of our day flew by. Lady Gray resumed her duties as official wickie, thereby leaving me and Milo with plenty of time to relax and enjoy the island. We spent most of the afternoon outside, though I was careful not to venture too far from the lighthouse. Every so often I glanced up at the stately building, confirming our direction and ability to find our way back.

The next morning Lady Gray woke us up early. The sky was still dark and only a hint of orange light could be seen across the horizon. "I think I should take you to the beach. I want to make sure you don't get lost. The captain does not like to wait!" she said while shooing us out the door.

Speed Racer arrived promptly at oh-five-hundred. Thanks to Lady Gray, we were ready and waiting. If she hadn't come with us, there was a good chance Milo and I would have been lost in the woods, going in circles, never to be heard from again.

My trembling fingers tried and failed to hook Milo into the zip line. Lady Gray once again came to my rescue. It only took her a moment to hook Milo in. He flew gracefully across the water, carefree and joyful.

As soon as Milo was out of the way and the captain gave a thumbs up, Lady Gray hooked me in. It turns out that I learned absolutely nothing about zip lining from my first adventure because the second time was just as bad, if not worse. I flailed around like a fish out of water, my screams drowning out the roar of the ocean waves. I came to a stop, upside down, my red hair dangling over the ocean, resembling a fishing net ready to vanish beneath the water. The only saving grace was that I provided my audience with lasting entertainment.

I am sure Lady Gray continued to laugh about my performance well after Speed Racer disappeared from view. As our boat raced away, my heart grew heavy with sadness for the island that I had grown to love, respect, and admire. A flicker of light filled my broken heart as I thought of my cozy mouse free home and indoor plumbing waiting for me in Greenville.

The day after we arrived home, Milo

commenced his investigation into the mysterious hidden factory. Word spread quickly and many people offered to help Milo gather evidence.

"Beverly!" Fable shouted out of his open car window as he drove up the farm's gravel driveway on a sunny, warm day. Beverly momentarily panicked, fearing she had lost the new Fable, the one she had grown to cherish as a trusted, dear friend.

"Have you heard the news?" Fable parked his car and angrily slammed his door shut behind him with such force that a shovel resting against a shed toppled to the ground.

"What news?" Beverly unzipped her white beekeeper suit and stepped out of it before hanging it on a hook outside a red barn.

"There is a hidden factory in the woods near the Greenville River and they are responsible for illegally draining it. This is outrageous! We have to do something!"

Beverly sat down on a green bench and took a sip of her iced tea. "Are you sure you want to get involved in this?" Beverly asked. She wasn't certain if Fable wanted to represent the factory or the fight to shut the factory down.

"Of course we have to do something. The Greenville River is home to many endangered species and it is one of the most important watersheds in our country. We cannot sit back and allow a factory to destroy an entire ecosystem!"

"Does this mean you are going back to work at the office?" Beverly asked. She pondered what it would be like to lose her favorite (and only) employee.

"Oh no! There is no way I am ever going to work in an office again. I love working outside on the farm!" Fable winked and gave Beverly a friendly nudge with his arm. "Plus, I love being your employee!"

Fable sat down on the bench next to Beverly

and pulled a bag of cheese puffs out of his pocket. Though he had replaced almost all of his old ways with better virtues, a few of his old habits remained. "We are going to sue the factory while we work here as beekeepers. Our bees need us and so does our community! So, will you help me?"

"I would be honored, Fable!" He offered the bag of cheese puffs to Beverly with a conspiratorial grin. She hungrily took a handful and munched on the cheesy, crispy puffs.

They spent the morning tending to their beehives and the afternoon working on their lawsuit. The sun was low in the sky and the honeybees were making their way back into their hives for the night when Fable left for home. The lawsuit was ready and Fable was going to file it the next morning with the court before returning to the farm.

Meanwhile, Milo and I started our heirloom garden in my vast, sun filled backyard. We followed

Lady Gray's advice and soon our garden was overflowing with beautiful plants that were loaded with fruits and vegetables.

One quite morning, as I was busy pulling weeds and attempting to avoid a wild, out of control garden hose, my phone rang.

"Hello," I answered, putting down my hoe and pulling off my gardening gloves. Milo giggled as he directed the water into an arch, splattering it all over himself. A rainbow formed as the sun sparkled off the water droplets.

"Hi Birdie." It was Charlotte, my assistant. "I know you are busy gardening with Milo today but I thought you would want to hear the big news! You may need to sit down for this one!"

I made the mistake of sitting down and immediately a stream of water hit me in the face. "Oops, sorry Grammy!" Milo laughed as he redirected the hose to the base of a tomato plant.

Smiling, I wiped the cool water from my face

with my shirt sleeve. "What news, Charlotte?"

"Fable Finch is suing a factory for illegally draining the Greenville River!"

"Fable Finch? As in the one and only Fable Finch of Greenville?" I asked, confused. The memory of the greedy, grumpy man momentarily blocked out the sun and I felt heavy and covered in dark clouds.

"Yeah! The one and only Fable Finch of Greenville!" Charlotte said with excitement. "He has changed so much since you were gone! He is a completely different person! He is noble, kind, and generous!"

"Life never ceases to amaze me!" I said. After saying goodbye to Charlotte, I took a moment to admire our treasure. The tomato plants were covered in purple, orange, yellow, green, and red tomatoes. The pumpkin vines stretched across every inch of the garden while the bees busied themselves deep within their orange flowers. The sweet scent of basil filled the air and, if I listened closely, I could hear the sound of the corn growing right in front of me. All was calm and peaceful, that is until my next adventure ...

68.5 million people were displaced worldwide from their homes in 2017 due to violence, human rights violations, conflicts, and persecution. Learn more and how you can help by visiting The UN Refugee Agency. https://www.unrefugees.org.[1]

---

[1] Refugee Statistics 2017, USA for UNHCR, The UN Refugee Agency. https://www.unrefugees.org/refugee-facts/statistics/.

Sourdough Starter

Ingredients

- 1 cup all-purpose flour (Plus more for future feedings.)
- 1 1/8 tsp. active dry yeast
- 1 cup water (Plus more for future feedings. Use room temperature or cool water.)
- 1 large glass jar. At a minimum, you will need a 28-ounce jar. The starter will bubble up and needs room to expand.

Instructions

1. In a large glass jar, combine flour, yeast and water.
2. Mix well with a wooden spoon.
3. Loosely cover the jar with wax paper.
4. Keep the jar at room temperature and allow the starter to ferment and bubble. Stir every 2 to 3 hours for 24 hours.
5. After 24 hours, feed starter ¼ cup flour and ¼ cup water. Mix well. Stir every 2 to 3 hours for 24 hours.
6. Feed starter again ¼ cup flour and ¼ cup water. Mix well.
7. The starter should be bubbling and have a strong, sour smell. If you are not ready to use it, cover loosely and place it in the refrigerator. Weekly, remove starter from the refrigerator. Pour off any excess water that has formed on the top. Feed it ¼ cup flour and ¼ cup water once for every 24 hours that you leave it out of the refrigerator. Allow it to bubble and come to room temperature before putting it back in the refrigerator.

Notes

- If the starter turns black, discard and start from scratch.
- If you store the starter on the counter, feed it every day. If you store the starter in the refrigerator, feed it weekly.
- The starter should be at room temperature and bubbling before using it in a recipe.

Sourdough Pizza Crust

Ingredients

- 1 ¾ cup all-purpose flour
- 2 Tbs. olive oil. Plus more for the bowl.
- 1 ½ cup sourdough starter
- 1 tsp. salt
- ½ tsp. garlic powder
- 1 Tbs. oregano

Instructions

1. In a stand mixer fitted with bread hook (or by hand), combine flour, salt, garlic powder, and oregano. Mix well.
2. Turn mixer off and make a well in the center of the flour mixture. Add in sourdough starter and 2 Tbs. olive oil.
3. Mix well for about 5 minutes or until a smooth dough forms. If your dough is not forming, add a bit of water or sourdough starter, 1 Tbs. at a time.
4. Pour 1 Tbs. olive oil into a glass bowl.
5. Place dough in the olive oil, turning to coat.
6. Cover with a clean dish cloth and let rest for a minimum of 2 hours or up to 6 hours. Add more olive oil if dough begins to dry out.
7. Roll out dough and bake at 500 degrees for 10 minutes.
8. Top with your favorite pizza toppings and bake for another 10 minutes.

Kirsten Usman is an attorney and the author of *The Case of the Disappearing Amur Leopard* and *Judge Birdie and The Meltdown*. She lives deep in the woods of Wisconsin with her husband, daughter, son, dog, and two cats. Though she has fought many battles with naughty raccoons, they always win the fight and eat every strawberry and ear of corn that she plants. Kirsten is blessed to have an abundance of deer, raccoons, foxes, coyotes, birds, rabbits, and honey bees as her neighbors. Learn more about her at PlanetProtector.com.

Thank You For Reading My Book!
Will You Please Do Me A Favor?

It would mean the world
to me if you could take a
moment to leave me a
review on Amazon.

Your thoughtful feedback is so very
important! Thank you for your time!
- Kirsten

More Books in the Judge Birdie Adventure Series

Judge Birdie #1   Judge Birdie #2

ISBN # 978-1732475601   ISBN # 978-1732475625

Made in the USA
Coppell, TX
23 October 2019